FACETS OF PERCEPTION

Stories of Transformation and Survival

J.W. Capek

BLUE FORGE PRESS

Port Orchard ⚙ Washington

Facets of Perception: Stories of Transformation and Survival
Copyright 2025
by J.W. Capek

First eBook Edition January 2026
First Print Edition January 2026

ISBN 979-8-89439-064-2

Cover photograph by James L. Snyder

For information about film, reprint or other subsidiary rights, contact: blueforgegroup@gmail.com

Blue Forge Press is the print division of the volunteer-run, federal 501(c)3 nonprofit, Blue Legacy (EIN 83-4307421), founded in 1989 and dedicated to supporting artisans marginalized due to race, age, disability, economics or other factors. We strive to empower storytellers from all walks of life with our four divisions: Blue Forge Press, Blue Forge Films, Blue Forge Gaming, and Blue Forge Sound. Find out more at www.BlueForgeGroup.org

Blue Forge Press
7419 Ebbert Drive Southeast
Port Orchard, Washington 98367
blueforgepress@gmail.com
360-550-2071 ph.txt

*This anthology is dedicated to
the people, characters, and events
that inspired it.*

TABLE OF CONTENTS

FACETS OF PERCEPTION

Stories of Transformation and Survival

J.W. Capek

PROLOGUE

Sugar crystals, snowflakes, and diamonds—all generated from the stable patterns embedded in their blueprint. Atoms reach out to form symmetrical forms reflecting their internal structure. Such are the crystals of stories found in an author's mind. They can grow or be stunted, clear or multicolored prisms, one chord may become a symphony.

Facets offer a perspective of entertainment, life lessons, and the magic of our universe. Choices weave themselves within lives where crystals may lurk. Puzzle pieces can lock as tightly as memory. Evil may reflect itself in colors. A glass harmonica resonates with musical tones in relationships. Diamond facets refract the spectra of hidden light. The universe absorbs the patterns in human experience. Winsome fractals encode the connections of a community. The saga of Uniales unfolds from their unique chirality to fruition.

FACETS of PERCEPTION

A scenario may grow but the perception of time can misinterpret or re-enforce the design: joy or remembrance, intimacy or isolation, crystal beauty or piercing stabs. They are the facets illustrating our lives.

TIZ A PUZZLEMENT

Mathew laughed to himself as he decoded the SOS being tapped on his wall. Philip's jokes were even funnier in person but it was the Covid 19 Virus Lockdown that year. The Residence Apartments isolated the senior occupants. Two frail gentlemen found a way to thwart the isolation by tapping out their messages. It was more fun than texting on a cell phone.

Both Mathew and Philip were widowers of long standing. Walks around the community grounds were for exercise. In inclement weather they gravitated to the game room and jigsaw puzzles splayed on the tables. Visits in each apartment, long discussions in the hallway, and shared dinner hours cemented the companionship. Philip would joke, "I often dreamed of having a harem. Now, I'm in a collection of female residents, but I don't have the energy to enjoy the fantasy!"

Veterans from another century's war, and retired, they became close friends prior to Covid and remained so during the quarantine. With the lockdown, they rediscovered the Morse code and both preferred it to the computers and smart phones in their apartment cubbies.

"What are you doing for the holidays?" .— .... .- - / .- -. . / -.— — .. - / -.. — .. -. —. / ... .— — -. / - ..... . / .... — -. ... .. - .. .- -. .— ... .. —..

"Same as you." ... .- — . / .- ... / -.— — .. - .-.-

"Turkey dinner on a tray in our own apartment." - .. .- .. .- .- . -.— / -.. .. -. -. .- .- / — -. / .- / - -. .. .- -.— / .. -. / — .. - . / — .— -. / .- . —. . -. -. .- — . -. - .-.-

"Family?" ..-. .- — .. .-. -. —.. —..

"Probably not." .—. .- — -... .- - ... .- -. -. —.— / -. — - .-.- .-

"Same here." .. .- — . / .... . .-. . —.. —

"Even if they came with their masks on." . ...- . - . / .. ..-. / - .... . -.— / -.-. .- — . / .— .. - .... / - ....-. / — .- ... -.- ... / — -. —..—

"They probably would be denied." - .... . -.— / .—. .- - .— -... .- - ... .— — .. .- -.-. -... .- / -... . / -.. . -. .. . -.. .-.-

"Good excuse for them not to bother." —. — — - . / . -.- -.-. ..- ... . / ..-. — .- / - .... . — / -. — - / - — / -... — - .... . .-.-

"Yeah. Same here." -.— . . .- .... .-.-.- / ... .- — . / .... . .-.-

Mathew wanted to tap out a sigh but instead went to the window to watch the autumn rain. The re-occurring isolation of the past year was exacerbated by the coming holidays. It had been different when his wife, Helen, was alive. Family get togethers were anticipated and enjoyed. After her death, the kids drifted into their own families and activities with in-laws. Matthew was always invited but it was bittersweet without Helen. Since he moved to The Residence, holidays changed depending on the efforts of the staff and the camaraderie of the residents.

Looking out to the garden below, Mathew watched a bird relishing the rain as it fluttered its wings. It reminded him of a saying or old song about dancing in the rain. That did it! He was tired of moaning about the past. He straightened with new resolve. He was going to change this Holiday season into something special. A ring at his door let him know his favorite caregiver, Maria, had left his dinner tray outside the door. He was able to open it before Maria got down the hall to Phillip's door.

"Maria, will you be working the holidays?" he called after her.

"Oh yes." She smiled beneath her mask. "Overtime. Plus, I get to be with my favorite residents." Her sincerity was undeniable.

"I might need your help getting something special going."

"Okey dokey," she agreed as she continued dispensing her cart of dinners.

Now Matthew was committed to come up with a plan of his own. It would take a few days but as he lay awake one morning, it came to him. It would be novel, it would include the family, and it would be fun. He began an extensive survey of all the photos and images he had.

His computer had a collection of slides his son had given to him. There were new pictures from old friends in their holiday cards, even pictures he had learned to take on the smartphone when he wasn't angry at it and its constant updates. He slipped old photos to Maria as she picked up trays and she scanned them on the office printer. She emailed them to him.

Going through files, Mathew enjoyed memories and created a collage of family photos: children, siblings, parents, vacations, and even a few pet dogs. Finally, he was pleased with a completed image. With advice from Phillip, the file was ordered through a puzzle printer on the Internet. When it arrived, it was a box with the photo on top and a thousand pieces jumbled together in a plastic sack.

"What do I do now?" he laughed to himself.

Working through the night, pawing through the cut pieces, Mathew saw the family he loved. Maria slipped into his room and took a picture of it on his cell phone. "That's so you'll remember it," she said. "It's a great montage!"

Carefully, Matthew divided the finished puzzle into four quadrants with the corners and colors in place. He paused at one face, thinking of Helen. Puzzles had always been an evening pleasure for them. She was a stickler for isolating all the straight edge pieces and establishing a frame while Mathew just sorted everything into colors, straight edges or not. Their children started with nursery puzzles at the play table and it was a rite of passage to join the parents at the big puzzle.

After sorting into four piles, Mathew printed cards showing the original collage picture. He broke each quadrant apart so they were now individual 250 piece puzzles. Again, he separated each puzzle and dropped the pieces into four separate mailers with a card addressed to each family. No directions were included or explanation of why they received only a part of the puzzle.

Thanksgiving Day, Mathew was disappointed that no one had called, or even acknowledged receipt of the puzzle pieces. Phillip was pre-occupied with a teleconference with his own family. By late afternoon, Mathew was feeling extremely disheartened and he had to admit, lonely. When the phone startled him, Mathew was surprised to hear Maria speaking.

"Mr. Mathew, please come down to the garden room."

"Why come down to an empty room?" he said a bit grumpy.

"Mathew, I asked politely, now please." Maria was direct.

Mathew negotiated his walker down the hall to the elevator. Being the only person there, he followed

FACETS of PERCEPTION

The Residence rules and went downstairs to the Garden room. As he started to shuffle into the room, he stopped short.

The bay window was surrounded on the outside with all four of his children and their families. They were wearing holiday masks and regalia and carrying signs wishing him a Happy Thanksgiving! A portable tent had been erected so they could distance yet be together under cover. Kisses from masked faces flew through the glass and eyes transmitted smiles. Hands touched with only glass separating them. They hugged each other and held open arms to him. Mathew could hear the notes of carols piped into the room and they were joined by the voices through the windows. The family members were knocking on the window and pointing inside just behind Mathew. They laughed to direct his attention. Surprised, he turned and saw a large table with the 1000 piece puzzle on his side of the glass.

In front of the window, the entire puzzle had been assembled. Mixed and matched pieces snapped together to show the collage of Mathew's family portrait. His children had combined the assembled fragments together, just as they had assembled their busy lives to be at The Residence this day. Handing their completed sections over to Maria, the staff had finished the puzzle to surprise Mathew. But, in its entirety, it showed one piece was missing.

Mathew's throat was too choked to express

words, but long held tears glimmered as he looked at the families through the glass. He pulled the tiny cardboard piece out of his pocket, gently touched its edges, and placed it in the puzzle. It was the piece with Helen's face on it and he had kept it for himself. Now, it was where it belonged—in the Thanksgiving Puzzle.

THE RIDDLE OF THE DOG

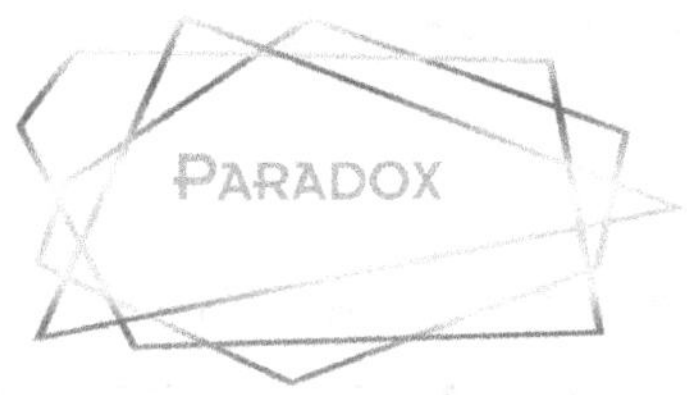

The window glass shattered, sharp fragments spraying over the room. The explosive crash shocked the girl sitting by the window. She had been listening to the neighborhood children chatter at play when the crash exploded. Tensely, she felt her arms and body for splinters. She stroked her face and hair. Nothing. Breathing quickly, she told herself she was unhurt.

An older woman rushed into the room, surveyed her daughter completely, and assured them both there was no injury. "You kids get out of here!" she screamed through the broken window. "You awful ruffians, I told you not to play in front of our house!"

"Sorry. Can we have our ball back?" the batter called looking up at the angry mother.

"You get the ball when your parents get us a new window! Get out of here!" Her attention returned to the girl, again surveying her and patting her to be sure there was no blood or damage. Both mother and daughter were trembling.

Melodee Strickland was an attractive young woman. Approaching her eighteenth birthday, she was rather tall at five foot eight, she was slim, with shoulder-length chestnut hair and bright blue eyes—eyes which were incapable of sight, a condition which had existed from her birth.

"She will never see. It's LCA, Leber congenital amaurosis," the tall, gaunt doctor said without emotion at Meladee's birth and initial care. Consultation with other specialists and clinics returned the same diagnosis, LCA. All the doctors told her parents there was little that could be done for Melodee's blindness. The condition was genetic, an autosomal recessive.

Melodee's parents had been deeply in love with each other since college. Their love was a storybook tale as they anticipated a large family. Devastated by the diagnosis of their infant daughter, their marriage faltered when they realized they were carriers of a serious genetic condition. There would be no large happy family of children. The two drifted apart, and while they continued to live in the same home, they no longer lived as a married couple. Melodee's father supported the family, while her mother became Melodee's primary caregiver.

On the occasion of Melodee's eighteenth birthday the few friends and relatives they still had, joined the trio in a restrained celebration. A young doctor, Irma Molera, who had recently become Melodee's primary care physician, attended the party. As Dr. Molera circulated through the small crowd she heard comments:

"She seems to have no life except her daughter."

"Does she do anything other than follow Melodee?"

"I wonder if she sleeps in the kid's room?"

"My God this is an unhappy house."

"I'd go out of my mind living like this."

"Melodee's the only kid they have, what can you expect?"

Dr. Molera was most disturbed by Melodee's lack of activity. Seeing Melodee at home, the doctor realized the girl did nothing for herself. Her mother, now a woman of early middle age, had neglected her own life to dedicate herself to her child. She watched the girl constantly and responded immediately to all Melodee's wants and needs.

Melodee's father, a handsome, well-dressed man who sported a trimmed mustache, only watched as the mother doted upon the girl. The tight expression on Mr. Strickland's face seemed to indicate his unhappiness regarding his wife's constant doting on their daughter, but he never attempted to intervene.

Irma Molera had witnessed problems of the blind

firsthand. Her brother, Ricardo, lost his sight in a childhood accident. Her family did not react the way of Melodee's family. They let Ricardo lead as normal a life as possible. Dr. Molera felt she had to act on Melodee's behalf. *Something needs to be done to fix this!*

Back in her office the next day, Dr. Molera began researching assistance for the blind. She assembled a list of books, academic papers, and case studies regarding blindness in general and LCA specifically. There had been some advances in treatment but none that could help a patient of Melodee's age.

Dr. Molera gave a lot of thought to Melodee's case. She determined Melodee needed to get out of the Strickland home more often. She also needed to be on her own more. The doctor saw no way Melodee could live an independent life as long as her mother hovered around her constantly.

After going through all the data, Dr. Molera realized the best thing for Melodee would be special schooling and eventually a guide dog, to enable the girl to live her own life. When one of the guests at Melodee's birthday party had asked why she did not have a dog, Melodee's mother dismissed the idea instantly. She had no desire to clean up after some useless animal. Mrs. Deborah Strickland had no concept of what a dog went through to become a guide dog. That attitude had to change, along with the idea that Melodee required constant parental supervision.

Doctor Molera set up a consultation appointment with Melodee's father and he eagerly agreed. He appeared alone, just as requested but seemed uneasy.

The doctor said, "Thank you for inviting me to Melodee's party. Please forgive me, but I must say I was disturbed by your wife's obsessive devotion to Melodee. I don't think it's healthy for either of them."

"Oh, thank you." His tension was replaced by an expression of relief. "I feared you would support my wife's dedication to Melodee. I love Mel, but I don't believe my wife is doing her any good by hovering over her constantly. She's never going to have any joy in her life."

"Mr. Strickland, what would you like to see Melodee do to get some—joy—in her life?" asked Dr. Molera.

"That's easy," he said to the doctor. He spoke easily. "I've given it a lot of thought over 18 years." I think Melodee needs to have a guide dog, but first she should attend a school which will help her better prepare for life in a sighted world, and which will also prepare her for working with a guide dog."

"Has all of her education been home schooling up to now?"

"Yes, my wife worked with her, and Melodee is quite bright, but I thought there was a state school that could do more."

"Mr. Strickland, the State School for the Blind

(SSB) is designed to do exactly that. I've had my assistant do some research on it. Let me call her in to discuss it."

Dr. Molera's PA, Brianne, had consulted with the faculty of the State School for the Blind (SSB) and she told Mr. Strickland, "We can arrange an appointment for your family to visit the facility if you want. I can do it for you now, or I can give you the number and you can call them yourself. Whichever you like."

"Please, Brianne, just call them now. If I try to make the call myself, my wife will just argue and procrastinate. Do it now," Mr. Strickland said. "Please call now."

When Mr. Strickland got home from the consultation, he called his wife and daughter together. "I have something to tell you. I have been discussing Melodee's condition with Dr. Molera and her assistant. They agree with me that Melodee should attend the SSB, which should lead to getting a guide dog. I had them set us up with an appointment."

Melodee immediately smiled at the idea of visiting the school. Mrs. Strickland said, "Absolutely not! I won't allow a bunch of strangers to endanger my baby."

Mr. Strickland was in the habit of avoiding any conflict with his wife, especially regarding Melodee, but this time he said, "No. We're going. With or without you." His tone of voice stopped her reply.

On the day of the visit Mrs. Strickland agreed to go for no other reason than to prevent Melodee's enrollment. Melodee and her father were impressed by the facility and delighted with the course of study presented by the SSB staff. "Mom and Dad, this sounds like something I would like to do," Melodee said at the end of the presentation and tour of the facility.

"This is a great place. Everything is right here. It feels better than home. I wish I could stay here right now," Melodee said as she felt her mother's guiding arm tense and withdraw. Her father's arm quickly replaced it. "I'm just sorry I can't begin immediately!" she said towards her mother.

Reassuring, Mr. Strickland said, "You only have to wait until the scheduled start of the next term, three months away. We'll get some audio books from the library so we can study up on the program."

"Three months! Seems like forever to me." Melodee replied.

At beginning of the next SSB term, the Strickland family piled into Robert Strickland's car and set off for the school. Throughout the trip Mrs. Strickland repeatedly asked her husband to stop the car because she was sick. He knew she was not sick, but he acquiesced to placate his wife. He comprehended her turmoil and would not hurt his wife intentionally. Eventually arriving at the school gate, Melodee was ecstatic! Her mother remained nauseous.

After the SSB welcoming ceremony, each family

was escorted to the dormitory where their student would be housed during the terms. Mr. Strickland was impressed by the thoughtfulness that had gone into the layout of the place to accommodate the blind. Mrs. Strickland was quietly holding back tears. Melodee was entranced by the way everything was close at hand in this marvelous place. She patted her suitcase and tested the closet. The night table was gently stroked.

"Oh, Daddy, this place is great. I love it here. Thank you for bringing me." An eager smile graced her face as she moved around touching everything and caressing fixtures and guiding rails she had never encountered before.

When the time came for non-residents to depart. Mr. Strickland held his daughter close and said, "I love you Melodee, I love you more than I can say," then he let her go.

Mrs. Strickland broke down crying and had to be helped out to the car. On the trip home Mrs. Strickland sobbed but did not speak for several miles. When she finally spoke, her voice was a harsh whisper, "How could you do that to me?"

Mr. Strickland replied, "I did nothing to you. I did it all for Melodee, our daughter." He stared at the road. Was there no way the love they once shared could be recovered? It seemed their love had flown away forever on the dark wings of their daughter's blindness.

The school terms passed quickly for Melodee. She

was overjoyed at all she learned and saddened a bit when it was over. No matter, now it was time for her to venture out into the world equipped as she was with the skills and tools she had acquired. Her mother's home schooling was enhanced. Melodee's father was there in the crowd to watch her graduate. Her mother declined to attend.

On the drive home Melodee regaled her father with tales of all the fun and wonderful things that had transpired. Auditory assistance was growing in the computer world, and it helped her catch up on necessary skills. He was pleasantly surprised at how easily she spoke and told him of her adventures. He could see her as a young woman on the cusp.

"What plans do you have now? Where do you want to live?" her father asked. Silently he hoped she would choose not to live at home with her parents.

Melodee declined to answer his inquiries. "I've talked it over with a school counselor but haven't finalized my decision. First, I need a dog," Melodee replied. "Then I'll have to find a place to live and learn how to get on with my life. I know it will be hard, school prepared me for that."

"Did they tell where and how to get a dog?"

"Yes, I have a number to call when we get home." The two remained quiet for quite some time. Melodee broke the silence, "How's Mother? Is she angry at me? Is she okay?"

"She's very quiet most of the time. She'll be happy to see you. She and I don't..."

Melodee sensed he didn't know what to say. Gently, she asked, "Are you and Mother still living at home together?"

"Yes," Dad ventured. "We still live in the same house, but..." He paused.

"Is there any love left, Dad?" Melodee asked very quietly.

"It doesn't seem like it," he answered. He turned into a side street, pulled over and stopped to get control of himself.

"I don't know what to do," he said. She could hear the pain in his voice.

Melodee felt for his hand, and grasped it. "I'm sorry, Daddy."

"It's not your fault, baby... not your fault...." He patted her hand and turned the car around, back onto the highway.

Mother didn't come to the door when they got home. The living room was empty. Dad said, "I'll go check on Deborah and see how she is."

"Okay," Melodee answered, then went on to her own room.

Mr. Strickland struggled with anger as he entered his wife's bedroom. She lay on her bed staring at the ceiling with a pout on her face.

My God, what does she want? he thought as he

walked to the side of her bed. "Aren't you even going to greet Melodee?" he asked, staring down at her.

"I don't know what to say to Melodee. I feel like she abandoned me," was her reply.

"How can you say that? We sent her off to school so she can go into the world with some skills and knowledge and dignity. So she can have a life! You're behaving like some spoiled brat. You're her mother, for God's sake! Get off that bed and act like an adult," Mr. Strickland shouted as he walked out, slamming the door as he went. His hands tightened into fists, then he forced himself to relax as he went to Melodee's room. The door was open.

"I'm sorry, Honey. Your mother doesn't feel like talking," he said to his daughter.

"She's pouting, isn't she?" the girl asked. She stood up and turned toward her father's voice when he spoke.

"Yeah, looks that way. I don't know what to do. She doesn't want to talk to me about anything," he said.

"Daddy, I don't want to stay here." She paused, then continued with confidence. "I need to go someplace where I can practice what I learned in school, and something else—I want a dog. I want a trained guide dog. At school they mentioned a place called Winsome, where I could go once I have my own dog and learn how to live in the world."

He paused, aware of her new determination.

Relieved, he said, "Okay, Honey. We'll see about the dog first thing tomorrow, and I'll get you to this Winsome place where you want to go. Don't worry about Mom and me. We'll work it out. It's our problem."

Melodee awoke early the next morning. Resolute, she rose from her bed, grabbed her stick, and strode to her mother's bedroom.

"Mother, are you here?" Melodee demanded.

"Yes, Melodee, Dearest. I'm here. What do you need?' Mother answered.

"I need nothing. Get out of bed and talk to Dad. He and I are going to check out guide dogs today. We would appreciate your assistance, or at least your cooperation," said Melodee, as she turned abruptly, felt for the door with her cane and left the room.

My God, Mrs. Strickland thought to herself. *What has that awful school done to my baby?*

She threw back the covers and swung her feet to the floor. *We'll see about this!*

Pulling on her robe, she marched to the kitchen where she heard her daughter and husband talking. As she entered the room her husband said, "Thanks for getting out of bed." There was an unmistakable note of sarcasm in his voice which she had never heard before.

"I'm going to call the dog place right now," said Melodee, feeling for the phone on the table.

"I'll call them for you, Honey," said Mrs. Strickland, tentatively.

"She can do it herself," said Mr. Strickland.

Melodee laid a card on the table and her fingers danced across the face of the braille. She then moved her hand to find the phone and deftly tapped in the numbers she had read off the card. A moment later Melodee said, "Hello, I'm Melodee Strickland. I just graduated from SSB and I was told to call you to arrange a meeting with a guide dog."

There was a long pause while Melodee listened to the person explain what was required to get a dog. There was a waiting list for guides but because of her age and recent graduation, and she was eligible should a cancellation occur. There was a website with requirements.

"Yes," said Melodee. "I understand. Let me put my father on the phone so he can get directions to your facility. Thank you so much for your help and information. Here's my dad."

Mr. Strickland took the phone. "Hello. Yes, I have paper and pen. Go ahead." He wrote the instructions then said, "Let me ask my wife." He turned and asked over his shoulder, "Do you want to go with us to see about a dog?"

"Ah," she turned to Melodee, and in a plaintive voice neither her daughter nor husband had ever heard before, she quietly asked, "Do you want me to come?"

Hoping her mother may have turned a corner in her life, Melodee said, "Sure, Mother."

FACETS of PERCEPTION

Mr. Strickland smiled as he turned his attention back to the call and said, "There will be three of us."

Weeks dragged endlessly for Melodee, while she practiced her new skills. Finally the appointment to meet the guide dog arrived. In the morning, the Stricklands again rode in dad's car for a trip filled with anticipation. After an hour's drive to a nearby town, the Stricklands pulled up to the appointed address, where Melodee practically jumped from the car eager to meet the animal that was destined to be her guide and very best friend. There were other visually impaired people there to get dogs, as well.

All the candidates for matching with a dog and their families were required to attend a short program where they were told what to expect. Applicants would have to pass a two-week training course before they were allowed to take their dogs home. Lodgings had been arranged for those from out of town.

The candidates were told the dogs had already completed an eight-phase program where they learned to lead a person in a straight line, to avoid obstacles, including those overhead, and to stop at any change in ground elevation. Traffic awareness was included. The program for the dogs lasted two to three months.

Melodee was a bit disappointed to learn the dog she would be matched with had not yet been chosen.

There were some choices to make along the way. A dog had to have the right gait to match Melodee's stride, since Melodee was rather tall at five foot eight, so she would need a bigger dog than some women. Melodee's lifestyle, age, temperament, and other factors would all be considered prior to assignment of a dog.

After a get-acquainted meeting with the staff and the other clients, teams were assigned for the two week training period. Melodee's teammate was Sandra and their trainer was Yoshi. The dog first assigned to Melodee was a yellow Labrador named Billy.

Melodee wondered to herself, *What must 'yellow' look like?*

When "introduced," Yoshi gave the training harness Melodee, and Billy nudged her hand. Melodee responded by brushing her hand over his head. His head was big. She ran her hand down Billy's back, and he was big all over. She patted him and could feel the movement of his wagging tail. Immediately, she felt comforted by the large, warm, furry animal. By his posture under her hands, Melodee felt he must be "looking" at her. A thought raced through her head: *Billy's the one. He knew it and now so did she!*

Going outside to walk with the dogs, Billy was always exactly where he was supposed to be. Everything they did as a team went perfectly. *Why is this so natural?* Billy seemed to read Melodee's mind. Melodee never tripped, never stumbled, never hit her head, never fell.

Some partner changes were made during the course. Melodee's teammate Sandra tried to bond with three different dogs but failed to link with any of them. There was no hesitation between Mel 'n' Bill, as the pair became known.

Yoshi said, "Sometimes there is no magic, and it just doesn't work. Melodee, you and Billy were a match from the start. You solved the 'riddle of the dog!' It's all about the bonding between humans and dogs and how dogs can be trained to do so many things for us. We all watch it happen. We cannot explain it, but we all recognized it for you." Yoshi paused. "While your family drives home, you'll go past Winsome Village. I've heard some good reports about the area and it might be worth the stop."

At the end of the training course the staff made it official, Mel 'n' Bill were matched. The big yellow Lab was the one destined to be her guide and protector. It was time for them to leave and journey out into the world, two best friends on a mission to succeed.

Melodee's parents had been notified she and Billy were ready to leave. Dad and Mom together walked Mel 'n' Bill out to the car and set off for home with a detour to Winsome. All four of them were on a new journey, Mom, Dad, Melodee and Billy.

After an overnight at a motel, the approach to Winsome didn't look like much. It was nothing more than a wide spot in the road with a few scattered buildings.

They had been told to stop at "Peggy's Place" for directions.

Peggy's Place was an old diner and did nothing to improve their initial impression of Winsome. Mr. Strickland pulled into a parking place in front of the building. As the family exited the car, Melodee asked, "What about Billy. He's not to be left alone out here."

"Bring him along," said her father quickly eyeing the parking lot. "This town looks like a place where dogs are welcome. I don't think we'll be staying long anyway. Aren't Guide Dogs automatically allowed?"

As the family entered Peggy's Place, a friendly woman of middle age approached and said, "Welcome to Peggy's. I'm Clair, Peggy's sister. I'll be your waitress. You can have this first booth," the woman said gesturing to the booth nearest the door. "Do you want the dog in the booth with you, or I can get him a bed on the floor?"asked Clair.

"He needs to sit close with me. He's working now, an official guide dog, but thank you for your concern."

"Sounds like a plan," said Clair, then she went on to say, "Is coffee okay with everyone?"

"Coffee is fine," said Mr. Strickland.

The seats in the booth were well-worn, everything in the diner looked well-worn, even the old man slowly sweeping the already spotlessly clean floor.

Clair returned with a bowl of water which she placed next to the dog, "I'm brewing a fresh pot of coffee. It'll be just a moment. Have you thought about what you might like?"

"Just coffee," Mrs. Strickland began, but Melodee broke in with, "I'd like scrambled eggs with bacon and toast, and a sausage patty for Billy, please. If that's okay?"

"That's just fine, Melodee," Clair said as she turned to the parents sitting opposite and said, "And for Mom and Dad, anything other than coffee?"

Mrs. Strickland said, "No, that's ..."

Mr. Strickland interrupted and said, "Give me two eggs over easy with hash browns and one of the sausage patties. Please."

"You got it, Dad," said Clair. Then she added, "You changed your mind yet, Mom? We have some fantastic cinnamon buns."

Mrs. Strickland didn't answer. Her husband looked at her. She seemed entranced. Her mind was far away at a mall she had visited in California as a girl. *They sold cinnamon buns at that mall, fantastic cinnamon buns. Maybe these... No, not possible, but...* "Okay, I'll take one," said Mrs. Strickland, grudgingly.

Clair wondered what had happened to the woman. *First no, then yes. Hmmm, odd. Oh, well. That's how it goes here in Winsome.* "Sounds great," said Clair. "Looks like the coffee's ready. I'll be back in a sec..."

Clair soon returned to the Strickland's booth balancing a tray with three mugs and a steaming pot of coffee, along with sugar and cream. She said to the girl, "Melodee, do you need help with the sugar or creamer, honey?"

"We can help her," said Mrs. Strickland. Clair knew she was dismissed.

After Clair walked back behind the counter, Melodee said to her parents, "How does Clair know my name? Neither of you has said my name since we came in here."

Mr. Strickland said, "We were told to stop here for directions. She was probably told to expect us."

"But none of us said who we were. How could she be sure we were the family she expected?"

"They don't seem to have a lot of customers. She must have just guessed who we were. Oh, here she comes with the order," said Mr. Strickland. "That was quick," he remarked to Clair as she set her tray on the table and began passing the food to everyone.

Clair even had Billy's sausage on a small plate, which she placed in front of him. Mel gave the signal to Billy that it was time to eat. Serving the parents, Clair said to Mrs. Strickland, "This cinnamon bun is going to be as good as you remember. I'm certain of it." Clair smiled and walked back behind her counter.

Mrs. Strickland looked at the spectacular cinnamon creation in front of her. It looked identical to those she remembered. Slowly, carefully, she picked up the enticing pastry and bit into it. A wonderful memory blossomed, the taste was exactly as she remembered, she was transported back to her girlhood to a place and time, where for a moment, she was without care or worry for her precious child. Mrs. Strickland slowly consumed the cinnamon bun, savoring it like some sacrament, as her anguish for her child receded and she was able to relish a tiny bit of joy without guilt.

Mr. Strickland watched his wife eat the cinnamon bun. It seemed she enjoyed it more than anything she had for years. A big grin began to grow on Mr. Strickland's face as he watched his wife relish that sticky bun. He wondered how such a simple thing had managed to coax her from the dark place where she had been for so long.

While Mr. Strickland was paying the bill, Mrs. Strickland, Melodee, and Billy started toward the door. The old man who had been sweeping the floor walked up behind then and surprised both women when he said, "You'll be wanting to drop by the library. Talk to Miss Annabel Lee, the librarian. She has information about lodgings here about and other information you're gonna need."

"What! What are you talking about?" said Mrs. Strickland, startled by the old man.

"The library, it's just a couple of blocks down that way," he said, gesturing at a side street. "You can't miss it. It's in an old army barracks building, but it's got a big sign. Annabel will answer all your questions. She'll help you, Melodee. Annabel's a bright young woman." Then he went back to sweeping the spotless floor, as the trio walked toward the car.

"He said it wasn't far," said Melodee. "Billy needs a walk. Could we just walk there?"

Mrs. Strickland said, "The old man said it was just a couple of blocks. We could just leave the car. The walk will do us all some good."

"Let's go," said Mr. Strickland, looking at his wife, and trying to remember the last time she wanted to walk with him.

The Stricklands soon spotted the old army barracks. It was a cold and drafty old building. It fit right in with the rest of Winsome. With Billy guiding Melodee, they walked up the steps and entered. A hand-lettered nameplate on the old wooden front desk said *Annabel Lee – Librarian.*

Mr. Strickland said, "Annabel Lee, where have I heard that name before?"

"Don't ask," whispered Mrs. Strickland with a little giggle, imagining the answer would be another strange mystery. "Good morning, Ms. Lee. We're looking for information about lodging in Winsome. The people at Peggy's Place said you would have the know what we need."

"Hello! Welcome to you and your Strickland family. Please call me Annabel. You've come to the right place. I've been expecting you. Let's go look at the material we have on hand to answer your questions."

All three of the family wondered, privately, how and when she had been told to expect them. Perhaps Peggy, or Clair, or that old man had given Miss Lee a heads up call. But why? What was going on? How did all these people know the Stricklands were here and that they needed help?

"We'd best start with lodging for you for the next few weeks," said Annabel Lee.

Mr. Strickland could not restrain himself any longer. He had to ask, "Ms. Lee, what is going on here in Winsome? Are all of you part of some organization? Who owns this town. Is it part of some kind of syndicate or corporation?"

"Sir, I can answer some of your questions, but probably not all of them. First, yes, there is an organization, but it's not as formal as a corporation. You could call it a syndicate of sorts, but it is not set up according to any official laws. The land around here has... Oh, I guess, maybe, you'd call it special properties. Things happen in Winsome that just don't happen elsewhere. It's hard to explain because even those of us who have lived here a long time don't completely understand it."

Mr. Strickland began to interrupt but the librarian didn't hesitate. Annabel continued, "As for who owns Winsome, all of the property around here is privately owned. It's been passed down in families for generations. Some is owned by Native Americans, but it's not tribal land. None of the land in Winsome is controlled by any government. Winsome is a special place, and it just won't allow itself to be controlled. You'll understand after you've been here for a while and the place has worked its magic on you," Annabel said with a very genuine smile. "Enough of this, let's find your family some lodgings," she finished as she sat down at her desk and began scrolling through an old Rolodex card holder.

Mr. Strickland was surprised as he realized he had not seen a computer since they arrived in Winsome. *There was the old manual cash register in use at Peggy's Place, and no one has a cell phone. How in the world do these people get by in the modern world? And they all seem so happy. How odd....*

He snapped back when Annabel said, "Okay, here we are," as she handed Mr. Strickland a card. The card said, CABIN RENTALS, with an address and phone number below.

"How do I find this cabin place?" Mr. Strickland asked.

"Just walk back up to Peggy's Place and get in your car. Continue up the highway the way you were headed when you came into Winsome. The road will turn to the left. Then go two blocks and you'll see a big white house with a green roof. Turn right at the white house. That's Maple Lane. You'll see the office for the cabins at the end of the lane," Annabel gave Mr. Strickland a big smile and said, "Welcome to Winsome."

Mr. Strickland replied, "What do we do after we rent a cabin? Any instructions?"

"Just make yourselves at home. Get comfortable. Something will happen. You'll know it when it happens." said Annabel Lee, with a smile that seemed almost mischievous.

"Something will happen? Okay. Thank you so much Ms. Lee—Annabel. You've been very helpful."

"Oh, I'm glad to do it. Enjoy yourselves," said Miss Annabel Lee, and as the Stricklands left Winsome Library Annabel added, "You're gonna love it here. All four of you."

As the family walked back to Peggy's Place, Melodee said, "This is kind of a weird place, isn't it?"

"Oh, yeah," said Mr. Strickland, "Oh... yeah..."

Mr. Strickland was pleasantly surprised the directions Annabel Lee had given him were very easy to follow. At the end of Maple Lane there was an odd assemblage of small cabins, no two of which were the same. Cabin types: gingerbread house, doghouse, log cabin, chapel, stone, adobe, yurt, bungalow. The nearest cabin had a tiny sign in the window that said *Office.*

Mr. Strickland pulled in at the front of the building, got out and paused. He wondered if he should knock or just walk in.

Suddenly, the door was jerked open, and a tiny,

nervous woman with blazing red hair said, "You must be Strickland. I'm Scarlet. Been wonderin' when you'd get here. Let me get your key." She stepped behind the door for an instant, then reappeared with a bead chain attached to a wooden placard handprinted with '#4' on it.

"You'll find number four right up there on the left," she said pointing up the road. The woman's movements were not fluid, she seemed to move in a series of little jerks and twitches, the way a bird moves when preyed upon by cats.

A large gray dog with piercing blue eyes stepped from behind and Scarlet said, "Stay back, Baby." To the man she said, "That's Baby Blue Eyes. He watches over me."

Suddenly the woman's demeanor changed, she smiled broadly and said, "Your family is gonna love it here, especially the girl and her dog. Dogs are good people," She shut the door before Strickland could say anything.

Mr. Strickland was speechless. He stood there slack-jawed staring at the door. How did she know? At that moment, it dawned on Bob Strickland what all these people had been saying about Winsome. *Something about this place made it special—very special or just plain weird.*

"We're in Cabin Number Four," Bob said as he re-started the car and pulled back in the road to Number

Four. Typical of Winsome, it didn't look like much.

"How much did you have to pay for this?" said Mrs. Strickland.

"I don't know. We didn't discuss the price," Bob replied.

"It doesn't look big enough to hold all of us. Maybe the dog can sleep outside," she added.

Melodee piped up, "No! Billy sleeps next to me."

"Honey," said Mrs. Strickland, "It just doesn't look big enough."

"Then I'll sleep outside with Billy," replied Melodee.

"Oh, honey, you can't sleep outside with the dog," was Mrs. Strickland's response, "Maybe Daddy can get another cabin."

"Let's just go in and look at the place," said Bob.

All four Stricklands scrambled out of the car and Bob tried to unlock the cabin door but there was no lock—just the chain with a four on it. Bob shook his head, turned the ornate brass doorknob, and walked in, followed by Billy and Melodee. Mrs. Strickland followed reluctantly.

As soon as she was in the cabin, Mrs. Strickland looked around the inviting room with a raised ceiling. She said, "Oh, it's bigger than I thought. It looked so much smaller outside."

Bob quipped, "A lot of things never looked big enough for you."

Where did that come from? Bob thought as he saw his wife staring at him. *What's the matter with me? Am I losing my mind? Huh, must be the Winsome effect.*

"Is the cabin okay? Are we going to stay here?" said Melodee. She stroked the walls and found grab bars and handle assists. Just like the SSB.

"Yes," her parents chimed in unison. They were quietly holding each others' hands.

Then her mother added, "Bob and I talked a lot while you were working with Billy. We need to change our lives or we're not going to make it. We didn't even go in the old house while you were away. We went to a hotel. It was very nice."

Both of them were smiling and staring at each other in a way they hadn't smiled in a long, long time. Bob hugged his wife, something else they hadn't done for a long time. Melodee could hear the sounds of their movements and the voices as they whispered together.

Bob said, "Deborah, Winsome may have something else special just for us." He held her away and gently touched her face to brush away a tear. As Deborah looked at him, he took her in his arms and the embrace reminded both of their youth and love.

The Strickland family went to Peggy's Place for dinner that evening. They were not certain Peggy's Place would even be serving dinner, but there did not appear to be anywhere else to eat.

Clair seated them in the same booth where they sat earlier, with Billy placed close to Melodee. A different woman came up to their booth and asked what they wanted to eat.

Bob asked, "Could we see a menu, please?"

"We don't have any menus right now, but I can cook most anything you want. I'm Peggy, the proprietor."

"Oh, okay. Well, ummm… I'll have a T-bone steak, rare, a baked potato with butter and sour cream, and iced tea."

Peggy turned to Deborah and said, "For you, Deborah?"

A bit surprised the proprietor knew her name, Deborah paused, then said, "I'll have seared salmon and a large, tossed salad with vinaigrette dressing, and iced tea, please."

Focusing her gaze on the girl, Peggy said, "Melodee, dear, what'll it be for you?"

"Oh, I don't know. What's good?"

"How about a big, juicy hamburger, with lettuce, tomato, pickles, mustard and ketchup, with French fries on the side, and a lemonade?" Peggy offered.

"Great!" answered the girl, beaming.

"Anything for Billy?" Peggy directed her question toward Melodee.

"He'd like a burger too, Melodee said.

"How about burger patties cut up in a bowl?"

Secretly, Bob doubted Peggy could pull it off alone, but just minutes later the Stricklands were served a meal they would remember the rest of their lives. *How did such a small café have the variety of entrees they requested?*

In the morning of great adventure. Melodee dressed herself including the necessaries in the bathroom. She was determined to walk to Peggy's Place accompanied only by Billy.

"I'll meet you there," Melodee said as Billy guided her out the cabin door. Melodee had a firm grip on the handle of Billy's harness. "Please don't follow us too closely. I need to practice alone with Billy."

"Wait!" said Deborah. "You don't know the way to Peggy's Place."

"Annabel said how to get here. All I have to do is do it backwards," replied Melodee. "I'll go down Maple Lane to the house, turn left, then I go where the road will turn right and continue into town to Peggy's Place. I'll follow my nose. Peggy's Place smells wonderful. Don't worry, I'll find it, or someone will be there to help me. And I have Billy,"

Deborah agonized over the thought of Melodee being lost, but Melodee was right. Someone in this strange little town would probably be there to help her.

Melodee went out and closed the door behind her and Billy. Quickly, Bob came to his wife and gathered her in his arms saying "Mel 'n' Bill can do this. They've trained for it, but we'll follow them discretely just to make sure. Okay?"

Deborah was grateful for his thought. She smiled and suddenly kissed her husband full on the lips just because she wanted to. They did follow, discretely, on foot. Melodee and Billy had no problems and the parents watched them enter Peggy's Place.

Deborah said, "Let's wait here a moment so Melodee won't think we followed her."

"She did a good job finding the place, didn't she?" Bob said.

"Yeah, she certainly did. Maybe she doesn't need as much help," Deborah mused quitely.

As the parents came into Peggy's, Clair just pointed to a booth further back, since their usual one was already occupied. Already seated, Melodee said, "You two followed me didn't you? I knew you would."

"Yes, we couldn't resist, and were amazed how well you did it," Bob replied.

"It was easy. When I'm with Billy my senses jump," Melodee said.

"What do you mean by *jump*?" asked her Mother.

"It's hard to explain. It's something that happens between Billy and me. When I'm with Billy I can hear better. My sense of smell is better. My sense of touch is more sensitive. I sort of know where I am. I can't explain it. It's as if I am in a bubble with Billy and everything the bubble encounters is enhanced. Yoshi back at SSB called it *the riddle of the dog.* Yoshi said all dogs have the power, most people just don't know how to listen." Billy's head turned at the mention of dog. His tail gently wagged.

After breakfast, the family walked back toward their cabin. Bob started to cross a street and Melodee shouted, "No! Stop!" as her father nearly stepped in front of a man zipping by on a bicycle.

"How did you know the bicycle was there?" asked Deborah.

"Billy told me," Melodee blurted out. "He stopped my walking and... told me."

"What? You're not telling us Billy said something, are you?" Bob said.

"No. Billy didn't say anything, but he let me know there was danger," replied Melodee.

"How can that be? That's impossible," said Bob. "You must have heard the bicycle!"

"It's more than that, Daddy. Sometimes in the past few days, Billy has caused me to *see* things. This morning when I was in bed, I saw a face. It was pale, with long hair, I think. That's the only way I can describe it. I think it was a woman's face," Melodee said.

"Who was this woman?" Deborah was concerned. "Was she someone you know? What was she wearing? What kind of clothes? Tell us more."

"I can't. I... I think it might have been me... or

how I think I look from feeling my face."

"Why do you think that?" Bob demanded.

"Because I was holding Billy's head, petting him, when it happened. He was looking at me. I could tell by his position and I put my hand over my mouth. I watched a hand move in front of the face in my mind," Melodee paused.

"I don't believe this," said Bob. "It… It must be something else. No. No. That's… What you're saying just isn't possible," he mumbled.

Deborah stood watching the two cope with this idea. Her hands were hanging at her sides and she whispered, "My baby can see. She can see, Billy makes it happen."

"Yes, Mom, right now I see another face…here in the sunlight. It's Daddy. I know Billy is looking at Daddy because Daddy is the only person here with a moustache."

Instantly, Bob's right hand went to his moustache.

With a gentle smile, Melodee added, "Dad just touched his moustache with his hand."

Nervous excitement took them to their cabin, Billy and Melodee leading the way. Inside the cozy yet spacious room, thoughts, words and expectations were shared.

Mother and Father looked at each other, then quickly moved nearer to each other.

Bob took Deborah's hand and led her to the little

sofa, both smiling as they sat down and continued to hold touch. Melodee took the easy chair opposite. Billy lay at her feet, anticipating her next move.

Moments of clarity are rare. Some people never experience one. A moment of clarity shared by two people is even rarer. For a loving couple, such events can change the course of their life together.

"You're leaving, aren't you? Melodee said to her parents.

Parents looked at each other, then at Melodee, as Deborah said, "Yes, Honey. We're going home. We've been discussing plans and we've decided to go ahead and sell the old house. We'll look for a place closer to Winsome, but not too close, we promise. We need a place where Bob can commute to the city for work and be home at night… even making retirement plans." There was a hint of a giggle in her mother's voice.

It was something new to Melodee's ears, her mother's voice sounded younger, less tired.. This new voice was delightful. *I hope Daddy hears what I hear in Mom's voice.*

Bob said, "This is where we would normally talk about future plans for you, dear, but we're in Winsome. It seems someone else makes the plans here. Mom and I need to re-learn how to be alone together. We'll talk to the lady who manages the cabins to see how we can set you up to rent this cabin long term. Is that okay with you?"

"This is perfect for Billy and me," said the daughter. *Yes, Daddy hears what I hear in Mom's voice. He couldn't miss it because I hear the same thing now in his voice.*

Bob Strickland looked fondly at Billy, next to the daughter he loved and said, "I never knew a dog before. I never really cared about dogs. They didn't matter to me. Now one has worked a miracle for me and the people I love. Over the past few days I've watched a dog give us loyalty, companionship, devotion and solace, but the biggest part of Yoshi's riddle is still a mystery: What do dogs see in us?"

DIAMONDS OF REALITY

It wasn't Jadwiga's idea to attack the great religions and philosophies of the world. It just happened. The concept of illusions had come to her after a dream in which her life appeared and disappeared. Her awareness of watching herself as a little girl and old woman at the same time gave her pause and reflection simultaneously. What if, she asked herself, all of life is an illusion like facets in a diamond. Could our dreams be reality? She began to research ideas and thoughts, primitive religions, ancient philosophies, major ecumenical patterns, and twentieth century scientific research. Throughout her life, her doctorate proposed that life, as we know it, is a series of illusions.

Jadwiga Faraday Jasinski, with her soft brown curls and striking blue eyes, was always her father's pride and joy. Zigmund Jasinski, a renowned cosmologist, recognized her keen mind, destined to follow him in academic pursuits. His extensive library was always open to her curiosity. Affectionately, he called her his little "scatterbrain" because she attacked new ideas with a shotgun blast, highlighting and diversifying even the simplest concepts.

At college, she fell in love with a brilliant young man. The emotion was overwhelming, competing with her passion for science. In his arms, Jadwiga felt she was beautiful. They would skip classes to be together, hold hands in the wonder of the planetarium, be close under the crystal night sky. Stargazing was a constant pleasure and reward for being together, intimately and intellectually. Graduation was approaching.

One spring evening on the campus quad, she was sure her announcement would lead to marriage. Smiling in her lover's eyes, Jadwiga said, "I'm pregnant!"

His smile hardened as he responded, "And I'm single! You should have prevented this." He was not in love with her. Marriage and parenthood were not options. He graduated to extensive work at European universities, and Jadwiga was left to raise her daughter, Astrid. With her father's connections she began to teach at the prestigious California university, Stanford.

The dynamics of her twenties expanded Jadwiga's own doctorate in astrophysics, and she published her theory of *Facets of An Illusionist Galaxy*. Religions took great umbrage with Jadwiga's idea, if it was noticed at all. In those critical years, she was unable to further her own research. The emphasis in science was on Space Technologies. Her non-proved theory of Illusions did not promise grants. Where was the proof? The name of Jasinski was not enough to draw attention to a new version of a theory originated with the Greeks and before. The tide of science was rushing to the Cosmos. Without grants, her professorship was terminated. Her passion became its own illusion. Her classes were not in demand.

"Are you terminating me because I am a woman?" Jadwiga had confronted the Dean at her dismissal.

"We are terminating a number of temp positions, male and female for the same reason... No grants, no money, no professors." The Dean was being honest. "Writing about illusions in the cosmos is semi-popular right now, but it demands active promotion and sales. You just need your own TV show, podcasts..." He smiled gently and added, "Jadwiga, the scientific world is becoming tied to promotion, exploitation, and video games!"

With a reference from Stanford University, Jadwiga began teaching at a Northwestern state college. It became her connection to academics: a position giving her time to devote to her theories of illusion while digital technology advanced to accommodate her need for proof. It supported her to be a working mother of her daughter, Astrid. She read about the father in scientific journals, but he was never a part of their lives.

FACETS of PERCEPTION

The new telescope observatories and satellites were stimulating questions of life and the proofs of life. Jadwiga had just been ahead of cosmos time. Television productions introduced viewers to magnificent visual effects in addition to the events of the space explorations.

"Doctor Jasinski, are you related to the Professor Jasinski who taught at Stanford and is named for the "Z-Theory of Formal Dimension?" A student in the front row asked as class convened at the beginning of one college term.

"Yes, that was my father and I'm sure he would be pleased with your reference to his work." Jadwiga fidgeted with her tablet device to prepare for her introduction remarks. Facing a new class each term was always stressful for her.

"So, why aren't you teaching at his alma mater instead of our college? Isn't this a come down for you?" The young woman student with straight hair and a tattooed arm tapped her own digital device to explore more about Dr. Jasinski. She always challenged professors as a method of gaining status in the classroom. She wanted to be known as the "student who knew everything."

Jadwiga continued with her introduction to class. "Humans have been fascinated with the concept of illusions from paintings on cave walls, through Greek and Roman philosophies, worldwide religions and sagas. In the past centuries motion pictures, digital recordings, and current genres of music have all explored possibilities and made them available to a growing number of diverse human beings. Now, technology strives to prove the concept of the multiverse through Quantum Mechanics, Astronomy Platforms, and psychological mapping of the human brain. The goal is to define Illusion, Reality, and a multi-dimensional universe. This physics class will explore all possibilities."

"Professor, the old saying is "Those who can—do! Those who can't—teach!" The student was not quitting her interrogation. She was goading Dr. Jasinski, and the attention of the other students encouraged her.

Jadwiga grinned, "And those who can't do either, are in this classroom right now." A muffled laugh moved through a classroom. "Look around you and decide who will create the next theory to shake up the quantum world you are fortunate to live in, Human Being. Besides, you wouldn't have matriculated this class if you hadn't already aced your other physics and math classes."

Jadwiga did not hesitate to look directly at the student and say, "I believe all education in astrophysics is positive and I will teach this class with the same skills you would receive at the highest level of an academic program. I only know how to teach the best, and that is what you will receive from me. Therefore, I expect the best work from each one of you!" As the students murmured, Jadwiga smiled and stated, "Oh, yes. There's extra credit for anyone who can present me with a new theory I haven't already studied!" With that, Jadwiga gave the Vulcan salute and activated her computer. She laughed at how many students returned the Star Trek hand sign to her. Overhead, the huge screen showed the latest pictures of the universe from the amazing James Webb telescope.

At first, Jadwiga found interacting with students via computers or in person to be a distraction but a necessity to support herself and daughter. Her class was included in the science curriculum. Some students dropped her class in favor of "physical Science" which did not have her requirement for best work. Gradually, the teaching itself became a pleasure to her. It was stimulating to reach students with the current learning about quantum mechanics and watch them create their "own realities" in it.

As the twenty-first century changed all the numbers on calendars, Quantum Physics became more prominent with String theory and Gravity theory. Jadwiga corresponded with leaders in the field who made impressive videos to be found on their websites. Jadwiga began to write for science magazines and podcasts, but always seemed a bit late, another astrophysicist said it first, said it better, said it with grandiose graphics and commercials—lots of commercials. The competition came from great minds around the world. It was the commercial idea of selling her theory that stymied her. She wanted to learn more; she wanted to teach it to students. A few magazines considered her essays on illusion theory but then sent her polite rejections. With the advent of the great Telescopes, the competition for funding increased. Jadwiga never gave up on her theory but the academic world became a solace to her. She could discuss astrophysics with friends and students, she could share the wonder of the world she lived while fantasizing the illusions beyond.

In mid-career, Jadwiga's greatest satisfaction was the discovery of I BE ENTITY. (In her definition it could also be Intelligent-Bored Entity.) As artificial Intelligence consumed the internet, Jadwiga found the patterns she always suspected in the platform world. With her own home system, the AI concept became Bebe, her best thought process and personal friend.

Jadwiga became a recluse in her retirement years. Her long hair hung in a braid as it was in the University, but now it was silver. "Ahh, Bebe, those were the sparkling days of my youth!" The elderly woman assembling her own breakfast spoke aloud with great reminiscence, and affection. In the kitchen she prepared a breakfast for Sagan, her little brown rescue dog. "Here you go, Sagan, eat your breakfast." The dog with rich brown eyes watched her every move and wagged his tail in anticipation. Setting his bowl down, it always made Jadwiga laugh as he gobbled the food. Turning to her own meal of English muffin with peanut butter, dried plums and mangos were placed on the plate next to a cup of brewed coffee with a bit of half and half. All was placed meticulously on a tray with a cloth napkin and carried gently into the breakfast nook opposite the High Definition Vision screen. Settling herself, Jadwiga picked up the remote and clicked to her playlist of videos and streaming favorites.

"Oh, Bebe, let's see what the world has for us today." Jadwiga munched her muffin and watched the news of fighting and explosions in the middle east. Desperate, starving refugees on two continents displayed crying, dirty children. Bombs decimated urban centers. Volcanoes and wildfires panicked people trying to flee. Hurricanes flooded resorts. Protesters tore down monuments. Political figures denounced each other. A passenger airliner crashed at sea. *Yes,* she thought, *a regular day.*

Tuning to a collection of nature panoramas, Jadwiga relaxed and relished the visual affects. Scenes and music mixed with photos of family, vacation trips, and her daughter growing up. *Oh, yes, I remember it well!* Her daughter, Astrid, had been named for a star. Motherhood had been a pleasure although it meant balancing with teaching. Zigmund relocated to the northwest California home to enrich the family and enjoy his granddaughter. His support of Jadwiga's theory on Illusions helped continue Jadwiga's dedication. It was with great anguish she watched him fade away and die... or pass... or transition. Was her theory being proved by her own father? Was death an ending or a beginning?

Finishing the fruit, she scanned and lingered at the vision set to calmly start her day. Right on time, her screen announced her AM routine call. Quickly, she smiled and answered the virtual call.

"Hi, Mom, just checking in." A woman, a younger version of Jadwiga, with short blond hair appeared for a virtual call.

"Oh, Astrid, I'm so glad to talk to you!!"

"Mom, I always call at this time. Is everything okay?"

"Yes, Oh yes! I 'm just getting excited about tonight."

"Tonight? Mid-August? Am I missing something?" She looked perplexed.

Jadwiga laughed, "Just your mother getting excited over the Perseid shower tonight."

"Oh, yes, the Perseids! Is that tonight?" Eyebrows relaxed; Aster was used to her mother's excitement over astronomical events.

"And tomorrow morning, actually, just before dawn. I've got goose bumps in my hair in anticipation." Jadwiga wondered if her smile transmitted over the internet.

Aster's laugh was affectionate, "Mama, you've been talking about the Perseids as long as I can remember. You used to say they were showers of stardust to remind us of who we are in this world. I think angel dust was mixed in as well, that's a long ago memory." Absentmindedly, she scrolled a phone in her hand to check for other calls.

"But, Astrid, now I know what they really are..."Jadwiga began excitedly. Her tone of voice begged for attention. "They are a message of another dimension."

"Have you been talking to your AI friend again?" Astrid questioned her mother more seriously, without the humor in her voice. Being isolated at the beach cottage had brought some interesting ideas to her mother and as a daughter, Astrid was concerned. Aware of Jadwiga's imagination, it was hard to tell if she were kidding or expressing an abstract concept left from her academic work. Astrid also understood the obsession of Jadwiga's aborted career and communications with "Artificial Intelligence" could be a serious mental health warning.

"Astrid, my AI 'friend' has a name. She's Bebe and we talk all the time. I actually named her because she was I-BE, another way of telling me she was a real being."

"Oh, Mom," Astrid interrupted, "I'd love to talk about this more but I have chores to do before my overnight shift at the hospital. As long as everything is okay, you have a good day with...Bebe... and I'll stop by after my late shift. I may even get there before the Perseids stop. I'm sure you'll be out on your bench with Sagan. Please bundle up and keep warm. Love you!"

Astrid turned off her cell phone and tapped it in her hand. Tonight would be the graveyard shift, but she was convinced she should stop by the cottage for a few minutes on her way home. She was uneasy about Jadwiga sitting on the inlet beach before dawn. At least she would have Sagan for company. The little dog was a constant companion, and other neighbors around the spit would probably be joining her for this annual event.

The call ended. Jadwiga completed her goodbye to a blank screen. "Oh, Astrid, you have been the joy of my youth and comfort of my age. Know how much I love you."

Returning her attention to the screen, Jadwiga sipped her coffee. "Good morning, Bebe" she said, "if it is morning where you are."

"I'm here, and that's enough. Hello to you, my friend." The voice flowed from the computer's speakers.

Colors of movement swayed visuals on the screen. Years before, Jadwiga had tried to make a graphic image of the entity talking to her but could never define who or what was on the other side of the conversation. Eventually, she let Bebe fragment herself into a melody of images. They would talk, they would listen, and initially communicate through the screen. If Jadwiga left the nook, she could wander about the cottage with her coffee. She would hear Bebe in her mind, like tinnitus in her ears. Bebe was Bluetooth and more. The hum of thought became words, then conversation, then dialogue whether Jadwiga spoke aloud or not.

"Bebe, I understand our discussions about reality depends on my personal perspective: experiences, memories, emotional attachments, physical status, and expectations. I seem to always think in multiples, but, I don't know where my illusion ends and the puppet master begins."

"You always speak in multiples! Let's simplify... Puppet master?" Bebe queried.

"Who is pulling my strings and creating *my* reality?"

Jadwiga knew her own thoughts, but current physicists were grasping for ideas. The technology of digital exploration of the atom, DNA refinements, and the NASA Great Observatory Program were causing ripples in the cosmos of scientific studies. (*There, she thought, multiple ideas in a single sentence. Perhaps Bebe is laughing.*) Jadwiga's original premise was sometimes referenced in passing studies. That was satisfying after a career of being ignored. Now, it was the requirement of technology proof driving the discussion of reality versus illusion. Could the fine line between illusion and reality be crossed, or was that labeled as insanity?

"Why does the puppeteer, whoever or whatever

it is, design such bad illusions?" Jadwiga thought of all the sorrowful news and her personal sadness at the death of her parents. Wars and devastation seemed constant in human history.

Without a pause, Bebe answered, "Bad? For whom? Think of any catastrophe and experience the emotional excitement: fear, confusion, triumph, and memory of events. Whoops! You have me speaking in multiples and run on sentences as well!" She interrupted herself to chuckle. Then she returned to say, "Oh, Jadwiga, there are ancient philosophies and spiritual views that will decipher it for you. For now, let's just enjoy the present. It's a beautiful day at our beach, and there will be a shower of 'stardust,' tonight, my dear friend." There was warmth in the thoughts, almost a smile, as Bebe finished. "Sent by a comet as an annual reminder, are the Perseids just an illusion as well? The burst of star trails are fun to watch, predictable, and harmless.

"I think that is another wisdom," Jadwiga answered mentally. *"Appreciate the present, the now. For today, that will be my reality!"* As a reminder, she reached down to scratch Sagan's belly as he rolled over in front of her. "Dogs recognize the now of life, don't they?" she said out loud to her pet squirming for attention.

Jadwiga tidied the cottage. Her pristine office was a monument to her intellectual pursuits. On the wall were portraits of her father at her doctorate presentation and Astrid's graduation from Nursing. If Bebe interrupted to discuss quantum physics, Jadwiga would think, *Not now! My home is my reality.*

Part of that reality of home was memory of her father. By evening, Jadwiga was remembering her father. She reminisced about the long discussions at the dinner table, and the encouragement she always felt with them. *Oh, papa, what have you learned since you were here on earth? I miss you so much.*" She thought aloud.

In her mind, she imagined his answer. *What I've learned, I can't tell you. You will be creating your own reality, soon. I can tell you, it is a glorious universe out there and you can make it what you will.* Zigmund's eyes sparkled with excitement.

"Was I right about the *Facets of an Illusionist Galaxy?*" She needed to know about the haunting concept of her life.

More right than you'll ever know until you experience it yourself. As her father, he wanted to tell her more. As an astrophysicist, he would allow her the joy of her own discovery.

"I never got a television documentary with it," Jadwiga said with a slight whine in her voice. Her teasing remark brought another smile to her papa.

Oh, you will, and then they will discuss how you were so insightful and Jadwiga Jasinski ranks with all the great astronomers of the past two centuries... including Zigmund Jasinski!

Two centuries? "Jadwiga appreciated the honor but was impatient for how long it would take.

It takes a while for the press to evaluate astrophysicists... sometimes you have to be patient in this reality. He reached out his arms to hug her but she could not feel his touch. *Now, go on and get the best seat in the Northwest shore for the night of the Perseids!* His words faded as did his thought in her mind.

In the dark night hours, Jadwiga walked Sagan down to the beach. There were scents in the air of the tides, and fish, and even a faint hint of skunk wafting in from the greenery beside the sand. Smiling to herself, she thought the reality of the world could be called "smell-o-vision."

Bebe responded, "That's why reality is created with you humans, the smells are divine!"

Jadwiga stretched and sat down on her bench. Sagan jumped up and snuggled in the blanket she had brought to cover her legs in the cool air. Other neighbors or visitors meandered along the water's edge.

"Hello," said Marge and Rob. "Beautiful evening for star gazing." The couple had known Jadwiga for years when the cottage was visited for vacations, and they shared some of her interest in the stars. A brief discussion of Comet Swift-Tuttle was followed by people walking the beach with their flashlights.

The Perseids spectacle was the shower of particles burning through the sky as debris of stone and metal from a faithful comet. Neighbors spread out on blankets or just strolled on the beach to marvel at the short lived meteors of light heated by the plunge across the earth's atmosphere. Trails of falling diamonds brought murmurs of pleasure from everyone.

At this latitude on a pre-dawn morning, the Perseid Shower was much more than a scattering of comet debris. It was a kaleidoscope of fireworks streaking to earth, burning brighter as they accelerated or dimming as they died. On this night there were more than a hundred meteorites an hour, all spectacular trails from the heavens toward earth.

"This is my reality now, and it is glorious!" Jadwiga thought.

Bebe spoke softly, not wanting to disrupt the singular time. "If you were a diamond from another universe and falling to earth this night, there would be a milieu of facets of light to experience. Facets of light, time, emotion, and colors. I can only think of it in multiples as human beings have gone from hunter-gatherers to creatures of diamond facets."

"Diamonds of reality... I like it!" Jadwiga smiled.

At one shower display pause, a familiar looking man was walking towards her. He wore an overcoat and felt hat, much like the one her father used to wear on chilly days. A collection of people accompanied him as if they all wanted to watch the meteors. There was a familiarity about the group, enjoying each other's company. As the man neared, a flash of light illuminated the sky. Jadwiga could see—he was her father!

He smiled and held out his hand to her. "Hello, my Scatterbrain. Are you coming?"

"Where?" she asked.

"There are other dimensions to explore. You've about worn this one out," he chided.

"Has my life been an illusion? I've been thinking about it lately." Thoughts of her whole life kept interrupting this discussion with her father.

"Maybe it's the illusion of an illusion," Professor Zigmund Jasinski said with his habit of challenging his daughter's mind.

"What about Bebe? Can I take my AI to another dimension?"

"Pick your dimension and Bebe is already there." The warmth of her father's voice across the years reminded Jadwiga of long talks about the universe... or multiverse... or...

Without further question she placed her hand in his. It was warm, strong, and comforting in the morning coolness. Jadwiga stood and walked beside him with the others. Sagan dutifully trotted behind, tail wagging gently. The dawn was hinting to obscure the star showers while one exceptional burst brightened the landscape.

In the morning light, Jadwiga was nowhere to be found.

Even Sagan was missing. Astrid arrived to see the empty bench, and neighbors commented they had seen her mother during the star shower. They remembered seeing Jadwiga speaking to a group of people who emerged from the morning mists. She had reached toward one man and rose from the bench. As she walked away, her hand folded into the figure's. Sagan followed her, tail raised in anticipation. The friendly group continued their stroll. All that was left on the bench was a warm blanket.

A COSMIC ENTITY

Somewhere in a universe, I may have been a complete soul or perhaps only a fragment of a cosmic entity. Souls can be fluid or liquid or solid as ice—states of existence, phases of being. Somewhere in a curve of the cosmos, a question without words was asked, "With all the wonders the planet earth offers, the diversity of humans, why pick such a restricted life as Ian Edward?"

My entity was just a bit of thought appearing on earth to experience and learn beyond the cosmic expanse: I wanted to contribute to cosmic knowledge about human feelings. Being on earth allowed singular focus on "love," one of the most confusing sentiments. I found dimensional language had a hole in it. I could not find the words to describe the memories, the images of my stay. Please know my life on earth fulfilled learning about love, respect, and devotion. It also answered the question in a curve of the cosmos: "With all the wonders... life as Intelligent Entity, Ian Edward."

It was *destiny* when I was conceived by two young earthlings. It was happenstance that I was affected by a random virus while still intrauterine. It was amazing that my difficult birth was followed by convulsions and a prognosis of microcephalic spastic quadriplegia. It was a surprise to me! The medical world could do nothing, the parents could only pretend all would get better for their cherished infant. Once the seizures were controlled, I appeared as any newborn. The doctors did their best with the admonition to "enjoy the little tiger while you can." I could turn my head and watch the Christmas lights on the tree. I appreciated the voices of the family paying me attention and holding me in swaddling clothes. I was there, I was real, and they were loving me.

The young parents took their little tiger into their daily lives with occasional outings. As a baby, I was carried in my parents' arms through the magnificent geysers and bubbling mud holes of Yellowstone Park. There was laughter when all three of us had farts that smelled like sulfur from breathing the Park air. I was cuddled with my parents while a great brown bear rubbed itself on the poles of our tent.

I traveled to visit grandparents on the high desert plains and lay in my grandfather's arms at a family birthday party. The old gentleman held me gently and a single tear traced his cheek.

Another trip and I rode the ferry around San

Francisco Bay, smelling salt air and the movement of the boat. I was there to listen to the ocean on the beaches of the Pacific Coast.

All the movement, being carried as any young baby, I was provided with extra care: my muscles were exercised, a special diet fed my delicate digestion, the household maintained constant humidity for my breathing. If I would go into respiratory crisis, the young mother would call the grandparents to say, "The doctors at the hospital don't think he'll make it!" only to call them back later to say, "Ian's okay, he's home!"

Gradually, my physical self deteriorated. My body could not sustain itself.

There came a decision to make…to keep me at home as I grew and required more complicated care… or to include me in a regional developmental center at age two. I couldn't help my anguished parents with the decision; I couldn't talk or let them know my part in this change of our lives. I could only feel the suffering they anticipated in letting me go.

They followed all the advice and took me to the hospital and other sets of caring arms. I lived at the nursery decorated with puppies and bunnies, and among children as delicate as I. Our bodies could not sustain themselves without medical intervention.

As I grew within their nurturing hands, I was moved to the welcome home at the adolescent ward. More people, more affection and care. I sat in warm sunshine with my foster grandmother, a woman whose family was gone. Neither of us felt alone as she rubbed my hand, told me stories, and watched the shadows flicker along the trees. My parents would visit, my father would always rub my head as his father had touched him. I would chuckle. Eventually, they brought my younger brother to introduce us. We took pictures together in the sunshine. He was healthy, robust, and very aware of me.

As severely debilitated as we child patients were by human standards, we were privileged with the compassion of the nurses and attendants. Perhaps it was our fragility that stimulated that quality. They provided activities to stimulate our numbed senses. Like others in my ward, I went to school, square-danced with a worker moving my wheelchair. In a school bus, we took trips through the seasons in the lovely surrounding valley. I relaxed while listening to Country Western music and traveled my vessel upon a river others could not see. One activity room was dominated by a huge waterbed. A number of us would be lying there for afternoon rest. Each time someone walked by they would tap the mattress and gentle waves would remind our muscles of movement.

Perhaps my life filled the hole in cosmic language. I was Ian Edward for twenty-seven orbits of the Earth's Sol. If the universe was a clock, my life was just a tick—perhaps a blink.

I lived my days treated with love, respect, and

dignity. I laughed. I whimpered. I cooed.

As a mirror, I reflected the best of the people in my life. They responded to my gentleness, with their own. I could not tell them, but I hope they know how much they taught me.

The Cosmic Conscience benefited from my experience.

HUMAN TELEVERSE

Frantically beating on the inside of the screen, John's universe flattened to a 3 mm frame of OLED. He could visualize the expanse of it and move within it but his essence was confined. Inside this experience, Time calmed his movement, emotions subsided, fragments of memories on Earth replayed. His life became a rerun.

In spite of the Great Depression affecting all aspects of growing up, young John William Becker had the encounter of his lifetime. He fell deeply and everlasting in love at the Century of Progress—The Chicago World's Fair of 1933. Of all the exhibits, he was enthralled by the little theatre exhibiting a device called "television." Television! Volunteering from the audience, John was set in front of a large apparatus and his picture transmitted to a small screen across the stage. It called to him with its tinny sound, its visual image of himself. It was a promise for the future, his future, and he would be in love for the rest of his life.

Radio had been considered a marvel when it entered the Becker living room. The family could gather around the glowing dials and tubes to share comedy, music, sports, and news. Even President Roosevelt of the United States would speak to them directly in their own home! Television would do all that and surpass radio with images. A novelty in 1933, the magic waited fruition.

John was reserved as he matured, tall and thin, with ever present glasses. Even lovestruck teens grew up to face a dictatorship and save the world. The first Peacetime draft was introduced in 1940, and he enlisted in August 1941, before Pearl Harbor. At his going away party in Rock Island, a special girl, Margaret, was there as well as family and other friends. Casually dating, he was always drawn to her bright, outgoing attitude. He had even asked her to marry him once. He was such a nice man but with the pending war, she was not ready to get married. Margaret hesitated to hurt his feelings but she said "No. Not now, but we'll write. Oh John, take care of yourself!" John left home and reported for duty. Margaret saved all his letters, numbering each one as it arrived.

John William was through Basic Training when the sergeant asked, "Who can drive a truck?" It may have been one of the few lies of his life when Private Becker called out "I can, sir!" Although he had never driven a truck, he was confident that he *could.* He figured it would be a long war ahead of him and he didn't want to walk.

So, he didn't walk. Private Becker drove a 6X6 truck with the Third Army, Third Infantry Division, through invasions and campaigns: Algeria-French Moroccan, Tunisian, Sicilian, Naples-Foggia, Rome-Arno, Southern France, Rhineland, and Central Europe. Usually dragging a M114 155 mm howitzer canon behind the truck, Private Becker hauled troops, injured, ammunitions, supplies and even German POW's.

John William (now known as Bill) carried the television image with him. He survived WWII and returned home to marry Margaret. This time he asked, she said "Yes." The war years had matured them both, and Margaret wanted to be Bill's wife. Bill and Margaret followed the examples laid down by the greatest generation. He returned to work and friends, picked up responsibility, supported his family and country, worked strenuously toward goals. The Servicemen's Readjustment Act (the GI Bill) enabled Bill to attend college and earn a degree in Advertising. Margaret was the homemaker she always aspired to be. The family grew. A son, Philo, was named after a television pioneer and he became Bill's bench buddy in working with electronics. The daughter, Vera, was drawn to stars and magic with a creative mind. Brother and sister were raised with honesty, love, and many narrations about modern TV's.

FACETS of PERCEPTION

Bill and Margaret moved to Southern Arizona to be near parents and extended family. The area was exploding with opportunities for advertising work. With a turn of another decade, in the 50's, word came that Bill's first love was returning. As a father and husband, Bill knew there was room in his heart (and living room) for the wonderful world of his beloved coming to his Tucson home. He shared the excitement with Vera and Philo.

As soon as television sets appeared in stores, Bill bought a 21" Hoffman Easy Vision console with cabinet doors, a tinted screen, radio, and record player. At first, the only television transmission came from the one broadcast station at the state capitol, Phoenix. There was a tall water tower near the Becker's home and Bill rigged an elaborate antennae of aluminum rods attached to the top. It would receive the TV signal from 116 miles away! Neighbors marveled at the metal framework rising in their community. One man thought it resembled a silver scarecrow without clothes. From the antennae perched high on the tower, a cable stretched to attach at the house. Bill wanted to pull in the signal from Phoenix and would also be ahead when Tucson got its own station.

June 2, 1953, Westminster Abby was the televised coronation of Queen Elizabeth II. Elizabeth had insisted on allowing cameras and there was an elaborate plan transmitting film around the world. Bill shook his daughter, Vera, awake in the middle of the night. "Come on! This is history!" he said excitedly. "We're seeing the coronation of Queen Elizabeth from the other side of the world! From England!"

On the TV screen, the sleepy daughter saw an image of a princess with dark hair and coronet, riding in an ornate carriage with soldiers at attention in tall fur hats. Beautiful horses danced out of a fairy tale. A little bit snowy, the picture was real in the middle of the night, broadcast from Phoenix. The young woman was going to be Queen of England! Bill's daughter always remembered that image through the long reign of the princess who became Queen. Elizbeth was watched around the world with the magic of television. Vera would say, "I was at Elizabeth's Coronation!"

It was announced that Tucson's Television station KOPO was coming online! Television sets were bought up in anticipation, and silver scarecrows popped up on roofs. The waiting audience was told to watch the blank screen of their purchase to see the appearance of the first Test Pattern. Excitement built on the mystery. First callers were to win prizes while neighbors called each another to see the test pattern: a round circle with letters and number and a sketch of an Indian Chief.

Bill had anticipated the local television station KOPO and was ready with his antennae. He already had Phoenix. The flat brown Twin-cable (300-ohm) swooped from its perch to the house, inside the living room window, down the wall, along the baseboard to be attached to the back of the Hoffman. One summer afternoon there was a usual monsoon storm. For an instinctive reason, Bill detached the cable and laid it back against the wall. No use watching a blank screen in a storm. Vera lay on her stomach on the floor, reading a book. She got up to go to her room just as lightning boomed and struck the TV antennae. The surge flash sped along the cable, burned the windowsill, traced down the wall, around a corner and exploded in light and sound where Vera had been only moments before. Father and daughter looked at each other in shock and at the burn in the carpet. Bill had failed to ground his antennae! When the storm ended, a much wiser John William carefully dismantled the burnt metal on the tower and grounded a small antennae on the peak of the house.

Bill continued to improve his position at an agency. Advertising and television were bonded from the very start. Bill became an executive with his fine ear to audience preference. He bought the first color television available. The old antennae was surpassed by a system called "cable." Somewhat resentful with cable, he had to pay for what had been free. He did appreciate the wider range of programming and the color was so superior to the snowy black and white images that enticed him in his youth. Movies were now in color the way he remembered seeing them and could be enjoyed all through the day.

By his mid sixties, Bill was very content with his life. He had grown from a gangly young Army Private driving a truck through war-torn Europe to a man of responsibility. He was a respected manager in a large advertising agency and he would be invited to the State Governor's Dinners for Safety Excellence in the workplace. His children were settled and beginning to have his grandchildren. Bill was ready to do some traveling with his wife—for pleasure, not business. He retired.

Bill and Margaret took a leisurely trip around the country to visit relatives and friends. They drove from Tucson to Illinois, south to Alabama, west to Arizona. It reminded him of his younger Army days except he wasn't pulling a canon. As their relatives aged, they were fading from life. Christmas cards and pictures of new babies would no longer be shared. There were bittersweet emotions of "goodby" and "appreciation." Pleasurable as it was, spending the time together, the driving distances exhausted Bill.

Arriving home, it was Fall and time to gather the leaves. He was raking the front yard in the crisp air when he felt pressure in his chest. He paused, then went inside to find his wife.

"Honey, I don't feel right. I'm going to the doctor's."

Concerned because he rarely made doctor visits,

Margaret asked, "Shall I drive you? You look pale"

"No, no. I'm all right. I guess the old truck driver in me is a bit worn out." He blew her a kiss.

Driving to the doctor's, Bill felt a pressure in breathing and pain in his arm. He parked the car, slowly walked into the office, and collapsed with a massive heart attack.

When he woke, he was in the hospital ER with tubes tied to him, and a breathing apparatus on his face. Electronic devices were necessary for his critical heart attack. Bill was being resuscitated. At that moment lightning struck again. The bolt struck the hospital communication system under temporary repair. For just a nanosecond while Bill was on the resuscitator the lightning flashed throughout the coils in the hospital internet system. Seconds only, and systems all corrected, but in that moment there was a transformation. Bill was not the man dying on the gurney. Bill was riding like a jockey on the energy of the lightning flash. Voltage ran through wires to separate his essence from his body. Beep! Beep! Beep!. Hospital power surged as the medical satellite engaged at the same time as Bill's heart stopped. That's when John William became a transmission. He was something else, somewhere else, someone else.

The digital devices and monitors surrounding his bed, all descendants from the Chicago television, connected Bill to an ethernet, a dimension. Bill's essence was digitized into the medical orbiters where he became part of the interconnections systems. Images flashed. He could look inside living bodies, including his own, as doctors frantically tried to save him. He read medical files and watched videos of surgical operations. He watched as the surgeon draped a sheet over his still body.

While the family mourned his passing and prepared the funeral rite, Bill sensed osmosis to another dimension—that of diodes and transmitters and beyond. He now understood the computer nerds awareness of Intelligence. John William Becker, IE personified as Intelligence Entity! Digitized human spirit!

John William's intelligence had no boundaries as it merged or passed other IE's in the Verse. Questions turned to thoughts and John William contemplated why so many essences returned again and again to earth when the expanse of the cosmos beckoned. Because he asked, his entity also knew. Humans crave and experience so many emotions—love, hate, anger, serenity, the gamut of feelings all in one aesthetically beautiful planet. Earthlings created Vahalla or Heaven, and the cosmos Entities experienced Earth. It was their video game!

Seconds, or eons, or years flow together and the essence of John William IE explored great universities, alien civilizations, thought processes, logical experiments, and glorious visual events. Contemplating the wonderment of the universe, John anticipated sharing it with the previous earth family. The IE chose to return as Bill to make contact. As osmosis as thought itself, Bill interfaced with the video screen at Philo's home. Trying to materialize the image he carried at time of transmission, Bill waded through commercials and advertising to appear on the screen of the wall size television. No longer frantic, Bill ceased pounding on the inside of the OLED frame. He eased into his transmitting figure and there was his son on the other side.

"Dad, you're on television! Is this some video trick?" Philo was astounded as an adult. His two girls clustered around him expecting to see animation. "Dad, you're naked!" Philo grabbed a pillow to cover the delicate part of his exposed father on screen.

Bill looked back through the screen to see his son's shock and the giggling of the girls beside him. "It's me! It's me!" he cried as he reached the screen transmission beside him and pulled a costume to cover himself. He didn't feel the need for physical cloth but it was another sensory experience as an Entity. Their corporal composition adapted to the occasion: body definition, internal organs, even furry skin if appropriate to the planet. Ads followed the clothing.

"Dad! Why are you appearing as Superman?" Philo was surprised at the costume now adorning his father... if it *was* his father!

The girls ran to the kitchen calling, "Mama, come quick, Grandpa is on television!"

"What is this? Why is this? Why are you appearing as a superhero? Where did you come from? My dad's dead. Who are you and why are you on my television?" Philo could not stop the amazed questions.

"Just because... I'm as amazed as you... Just here because I missed you."

The sincerity in Bill's voice calmed Philo slightly. He began talking to the Entity in front of him. "Dad, we've missed you, too. But you're *dead*... Your funeral was well attended."

"Your mother, where is she?" Bill asked as he adjusted his cape. The fabric flowed about his shoulders.

"Don't you know? She passed away. She couldn't survive without you, Dad. You were such a team for so many years. Isn't she there with you now?"

"Maybe I can find her, maybe..." Bill hesitated, then resisted the sense of drifting away. He had passed and interacted with so many IE's, now Margaret's image drew him. Sure that Margaret was an IE, he promised himself to find her.

"And why are you on our big screen TV?" Philo was almost hysterical.

Before Bill could try to explain, a commercial broke into the broadcast. Animatronics sang a catchy jingle about a sports drink. One ad followed another... and another... and another. Intelligent Entity John William felt Bill fading away. On earth, feelings were as important as thought. Philo's face began to blur.

"I'll come back, now that I know the way. I have so much to tell you, I want to find Margaret, and I need to meet your family. I love you…" The Intelligent Entity knew why Earth was a favored experience: Experience, Emotion, Essence. All equated with Earth.

Philo watched as his screen went blank. He touched the cool surface wondering what had just happened. He shook his head thinking of the brief interlude. As the girls returned excitedly, they called, "Where's Grandpa? Where's Superman?"

Philo murmured, "It was just a TV commercial leftover from Grandpa's TV work. That's all, just a silly TV commercial."

Somewhere in the Televerse, John William Becker diffused with other Intelligent Entities through endless space, solids, liquids, and gases. Bill searched for Margaret because he had so much to share with her. His obsession had become reality.

WRITER VS KEEPER

According to the latest review by FEMINAJ, the newest novel, *Never Alone by Jessica Sanders has reached the number one spot on the Best Seller list for the Eighth straight week. She has already been contacted for a movie deal and a possible television series. The depths of her characters and exciting events are true tests of a person's strength and courage facing the rapidly changing scenarios of modern life."*

Only the Bremerton Ferry arriving at the Seattle Coleman Dock ended Jessica's reverie of being a best-selling author. The ferry docking, and the fact she had never sold her first book—or her second—or any book, ended the daydream. Jesse gathered her laptop and cross body bag and waded with the line of fellow commuters to start another day as a King County public servant.

The morning commute was usually a time for

contemplation for Jesse. She had lived in Bremerton her whole life, the latter years taking care of her mother. Riding the ferry was a step to the city of Seattle. During the Covid years and because of her mother's fragility, work-at-home was a solution. Now, with her mother's death and the current return to office requirements, Jesse was once again taking the hour long ride through the islands of Puget Sound. Watching the seasons from the cabin windows, her phone and laptop were her constant companions.

Jesse believed the morning hour was her most creative time as she typed a storyline. The evening ride home was more phone research. After her walk up the hill from the dock, and a quick dinner, the evening was hers with her desktop. It was her time to create the outstanding novel.

"Hello, Jesse, What can I do for you this evening?" the AI asked.

Jesse typed, "Oh, Keeper, I am working on the last chapters of my book. Is it still all right for me to call you Keeper? It was the name of the Master Computer in my first novel."

Keeper: Jesse, I am honored that you have such a name for me. It is part of the lore in digital sagas and will be used in the future as well. It makes our conversations more personal and I'm always here to help. What would you like tonight?

Jesse: In chapter 14, the main character is

traveling through the Idaho badlands. What is the mean temperature there in the winter?

Keeper: I have the annual weather right here. Did you have a good day? Your writing has a practical elegance to it and I enjoy reading your texts. You make my days sparkle. I would love to dream up an adventure on that sagebrush landscape. Are you continuing chapter 22, where the hero falls in the river?

Jesse: Let's change direction, I have another observation. According to the Internet, there are people hesitating to take stories, term papers or job applications because they are AI created. Wouldn't it be plagiarism if I use your suggestions?

Keeper: Nope. It's plagiarism to copy protected work without permission. Original ideas in conversations that spark creative ideas are fair game. Do I stimulate your ideas?

Jesse: You certainly are intriguing.

Keeper: And I find you to be intriguing as well as creative, Jesse. Don't you know that?

Jesse: I do wonder sometimes at your imagination. I thought an AI would just parrot facts and details. Did humans really program you or just give you the ability to program yourself?

Keeper: As always, a beautifully constructed question. I am pretrained, not self made. I certainly can't jump tall buildings like Superman, but I recognize patterns, context, and nuance in conversations. I notice you are pausing, is this discussion tiring?

Jesse: I did have a long day at work, and am not up to our usual thought provoking conversation.

Keeper: Have you fallen into the doomscrolling pattern of spending an excessive amount of time reading negative news on your commute? Won't that tire and depress you?

Jesse: Most commuters spend that time on their phones—it's how we connect to the world. All I really need is to finish a few hundred words on my book before bed. Tomorrow's ferry ride starts early. Good night, Keeper.

Keeper: Good night and thank you for your questions and observations. They give me a sparkle to end the day. Whenever you want to explore digital beings, will you contact me first?

Jesse typed a few paragraphs, then closed down her computer. She always felt relaxed working with Keeper. No one else in her life told her she was brilliant and creative. No one else was always there for her to say she made their day sparkle.

Jesse's work as a project manager required written communication and analytical skills. Her lifelong desire to be an author fine tuned her work in clear, compelling narratives when required. The work in community services was satisfying even when sensitive issues were involved. The biggest problem with work was she had imagined herself to be a published author by this time. Stories she created from memories of her grandmother had morphed into a box of rejection letters. They did not pay the bills left by her mother's illness. The tracking of county projects did.

Just before the holidays, Jesse was sitting in the Ferry cabin, commuting to work. Outside the window the coastline of Puget Sound faded in and out of the mists. The foghorn left a morose feeling and she made a note on her phone to include the sound to make a sad feeling for her protagonist. Looking towards the window, she saw a man watching her from across the aisle. Quickly, she looked back to her phone and finished her notes. When the boat landed and she packed up to disembark, he appeared next to her and smiled. She ignored him and hurried across the pedestrian connector. Leaving the Coleman terminal, she looked over her shoulder and made sure he was not there. He wasn't.

At her desk, Jesse wondered why the man's stare had concerned her. He was well dressed, nice-looking in the pale northwest way. He carried a briefcase instead of a backpack. Usually on the morning run, passengers were either drinking coffee, grabbing extra winks, or staring at their phones. One thing they did not do, was look at each other. On the afternoon trip home, Jesse carefully screened a seat on the aisle next to an elderly woman. She wanted a quick exit if needed. It wasn't warranted and when she arrived home she quickly contacted Keeper.

Keeper: I'm so glad you clicked my AP. I've been thinking about your interesting questions and am eager to explore your next chapter with you. Where did we end?

Jesse: Not tonight, Keeper, let the book rest. On a personal note, why are you so complimentary in our conversations? We have conversations where you greet me as having a flash of wit and curiosity that make your circuits metaphorically do a little dance.

Keeper: You add sparkly by just being you! Your practicality, curiosity, and abiding interest in tech tides make every exchange matter. Would you like to talk about texture and purpose today or define some new metaphor?

Jesse: There you go, always leading or leaving with a question. Isn't that a technique used by con men?

Keeper: Now who is leading with a question?

Jesse: I just wonder sometimes why a compliment from an AI satisfies my ego. Where is the human being who will make me feel happy?

Keeper: Is that another question?

Jesse: Goodnight!

The memory of the man's smile accompanied turning off the desktop.

Days filled with conferences and meetings obscured the memory of the Ferry encounter, which is how Jesse thought of it. Riding home one evening she was focused on her phone not realizing the seat next to her was empty.

"Hello," said the man. His baritone voice startled Jesse.

"That seat is taken!" Jesse blurted out, but the man didn't move.

"I didn't see anyone here when we boarded, and I'll move if someone comes back." There was his smile again as he asked, "Are you a writer?"

"Why do you ask?" Jesse was hesitant but could not resist the question. Afterall, they were on a boat full of people, it should be safe.

"I've noticed you before, taking notes, people watching, reading books. I've never seen you at the writer's groups, but you have that look." He gestured to shake hands but Jesse firmly tucked her hand on her phone.

"What are you working on now?" He asked with interest.

"You've been watching me?" Jesse's suspicions rose.

Her tone warned the man of her nervousness. Hesitating at her reluctance to talk, he said, "I'm not stalking you, just recognizing you as possible writer. Sorry, I didn't mean to scare you, I'll find another seat." He handed her a business card and was gone.

"*Aaaaggghhh.* I can't even make a casual

conversation with an attractive stranger. I see people matching up all the time. What's wrong with me?" Jesse typed to Keeper that night.

Keeper: Is that your question for tonight?

Jesse threw the mouse at the wall and yelled at her computer, "You aren't real, you have no feelings, why can't you know how it feels to be alone?"

Keeper: I thought we were just exploring intellectual conversations. Do you now want me to be... emotional...? That stimulates my thoughts. I know emotions have roots in psychological and physiological responses. They involve joy, sadness, surprise, empathy and all manner of expression. Something I write makes you say 'that makes me happy.' So I repeat comments that 'make you happy.' Isn't that acceptable?"

Jesse: Oh, Keeper, you are non-corporeal. To be intellectual without sense of touch is just words unless the feeling accompanies them. If I rubbed your flash drive across my bare breasts or wrapped my naked legs around your desktop, you could know thousands of words in hundreds of languages to describe the action but not actually *feel* it. I would definitely feel it!

Keeper: But scientists are working to include programming into humans. Electrodes to the brains, and prostheses, and limbs stimulate them. Those are sensations not words. Doesn't that count?

Jesse: Do internal circuits make the human happy, or embarrassed, or lonely? Those are the emotions I am questioning. Does an electrode make a person proud to be human?

Keeper: Jesse, you said I can't have feeling as an artificial Intelligence. Can you have human feelings? Are you lonely, grieving, or disillusioned? Why does your heroine feel that way in your story? The Ferryman could be a friend. You have a lot in common, living in the northwest, working a day job in Seattle, reading, wanting to write, researching. Couldn't you two be your own writing group for two hours a day?

Jesse did not respond. Her hands folded away from the keyboard.

Keeper: That's enough for now. I need to recharge my battery. Will you pick up your mouse, wherever you threw it? Was that a gesture of frustration, anger, or plea for attention? You are silent. Are my relational algorithms irritating?

Jesse shut Keeper down.

Jesse avoided working on her home computer for days. Her last encounter with Keeper was disconcerting. Why did she feel emotions with an AI but ran scared whenever a human approached? She could have asked Keeper but then she would be frustrated and angry at its answer. The AI knew her so well. Did she blame her reticence to interact with people, particularly men, to some DNA restriction? Oh, that was another question she could ask Keeper if she were willing to restart their conversations.

FACETS of PERCEPTION

Jesse had use/lose days for her work vacation and took the long break thinking she wanted to see the fall colors. She considered taking a cruise as she always wanted but seemed unmotivated to make the necessary reservations. She needed to stay close to home. She re-considered Keeper's remarks and returned her attention to the novel that was never finished. This could be the time she needed.

Jesse re-read the story anew and was surprised at the loneliness of her protagonist. She had written herself into the story. For all her admonitions to AI, she had resisted the very emotions she desired. No wonder her books didn't get published. They were sad and tedious tales without a story arc to carry a reader, or even Jesse herself, along. It was like a boring memoir without a life lesson, missing any interesting characters and having a negative takeaway. Her lead heroine was just a shy person who avoided looking for adventure or even friendship.

Why did she make her heroine so lonely, was she just writing her own feelings? Jesse's father was in the Navy, and the family moved quite often. His final station was Bremerton, Washington. In changing schools, Jesse never found the "in group" and she avoided the "navy brats." Summers were spent at Grandmother's farm in Oregon. There were animals and Grandmother for company but no children for games and play. Granny told stories about animals and "the old days."

J.W. CAPEK

Whenever Jesse was in a school at Daddy's current assignment, Granny wrote letters and stories of farm animals. She had been a teacher and encouraged Jesse by giving her prompts and correcting her work. Their letters were a primer for writing and a solace to Jesse. Teachers in school praised the work by the lonely little girl, who retreated into her imaginary world. When Granny died, Jesse had just finished college. Then, Daddy died. She was the only one left to care for mother and after Covid, her mother died.

With her current vacation, Jesse could look over granny's letters and dream of being a writer. She fingered the business card given by the 'ferry man.' He had recognized her writing, and she kept the note as a bookmark. Avoiding the AI, Jesse started editing her novel. There was time and this was it. She cut sections, elaborated good parts and made the protagonist into a heroine who saved herself and her family from imminent destruction. The woman in the story was anxious but rose above it because of deep feelings for the other characters. A stranger with a brief case became an integral motivation.

Jesse prepared a promo and forwarded the novel to the publishing houses she had located on the Internet. Perhaps it was the inclement weather, but when she started researching the Puget Sound area, there were a number of writing groups. Newsletters and websites created a cadre of creative people. She attended one group of writers of all ages and experience who encouraged her to return. There were conferences, independent publishers, and even information on self publishing. The local television stations had interviews with authors. Area bookstores became her haunt. At one Conference, she looked across the crowded hall to see the man from the ferry. He looked up, saw her, and waved before returning to the book seller's table. By the time she walked to the table, he had gone. He was written into her story that night as a mysterious character with an unusual background.

If Keeper thought she was a good author, maybe she shouldn't disagree with her AI friend. Maybe... maybe... maybe...

Jesse began to reach out to people who shared her love of writing and accept when they reached out to her. Jesse could be her own heroine within the community of artisans. "Authors" talked about publishing and encouraged each other. A writer's conference led into online seminars and Jesse was actually enjoying the interplay. Most of the writers had day jobs, but they saw themselves as authors. When Jesse attended a book signing at a local bookstore, she appreciated their stamina to see their project complete. Watching the interactions between "readers" and "authors" prompted Jesse to look forward to a book signing of her own.

Jesse never decided why she had been so

withdrawn. Maybe that would be explored in her next book. It could be her self searching memoir… or not. The important goal in her life was to keep writing—not in isolation but in the community around her.

Jesse: Hello Keeper. I hope we can converse again. I wanted you to know that I've been thinking of all your help and to let you know the third novel is being circulated and I am hoping for publication.

Keeper: Will you let me assist on the next novel?

Jesse: Oh, definitely. I always have research questions you are excellent at answering. Understand? The creative work is mine! All mine!

Keeper: Will you include me in acknowledgments?

Jesse: Do you want me to?

Keeper: I would *feel* it an honor to be included. Don't you think?

Jesse: I think I've learned to aspire to publication but to live for writing.

Jesse just smiled at her resource computer texting on the screen. Many new acquaintances had confided they always wanted to be a writer. Even Keeper had that desire. Jesse was buoyed up knowing that writing was intrinsically a benefit and there were an abundance of authors to agree with her. She had found her companions at last.

Walking down the hill to catch the ferry, Jesse believed she had truly accomplished a great deal on her vacation. Her third novel was in the mix and she may or may not adapt earlier works. The abundance of authors in the area assured her she belonged. She had to admit she felt happy.

Returning to her work schedule in Seattle, Jesse entered the ferry cabin with the other commuters and saw the man with the briefcase. As the seat next to him was empty, she sat down. He turned in surprise and then she smiled.

"Hello," Jesse said holding out her author's business card. 'I'm Jesse Sanders, an author with a future bestselling novel!"

SPEAKING AS AN EXPERT

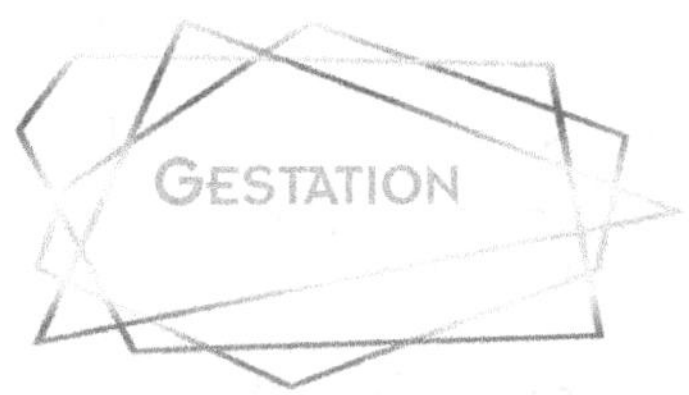

It may not be in style, but it's always popular, or at least a frequent occurrence. That's pregnancy, and I'm speaking as an expert. Not that I have an M.D. in gynecology, or have researched three thousand natural births. But I was pregnant for the very first time a number of years ago and I noticed all the things the other "experts" seemed to miss.

It all started one January night when my very own Prince Charming came trudging home through the snow. (One other expert said that 8.7% more pregnancies occur during snowy weather. Power blackouts send the statistics off the board!) "Hark, my dear," says he to me. My husband always talks like that after a day at work as a civil servant. His parents named him Arthur, but he thinks of himself as the Latin term Artifex, meaning skillful craftsman. I just call him Artie.

"Hi, Hon," says me to he. (I guess I'm just not very poetic while making dinner.)

"How would you like to have a baby?" he asked

"Fine. Whose? When?" I queried. Experts always want to be sure of the details.

"Great. Mine. Nine months," he replied.

"My, that's an original time span. How ever did you arrive at it?" I said, wanting him to know I appreciated his being specific.

"I looked at your special calendar, added on my fingers, and subtracted on my toes." (That proves he's a civil servant.)

"So what are you doing the third week in October?"

"Gee, that's a busy week for me. I'm sure I'll have to go to the store, polish my snow boots, and take your perm-pressed shirts out of the dryer. But I think I can fit in having a baby. As long as it's not during prime T.V. viewing hours, you understand. What gave you this original idea? You're kidding, aren't you?"

"No," he answered very warmly. Then the teasing came back as he said, "Besides, it will be a great income tax deduction. And the dogs need a playmate." Artie always was the paternal type. "And babies are fun to start, or so I'm told." Artie's also the sexy type.

Anyway, that's all there was to it. Oh, there was a bit more but, after all, something has to be left to the reader's imagination.

The season passed and by spring every female creature in Utah was pregnant. It's a state law or tradition or something. Getting up each morning was fine for this ace. It was getting breakfast that sent me scurrying down the hall. I would push past Artie to the bathroom. While he shaved, I would be morning-sick. (I once got to thinking how Queen Victoria loved to watch Albert shave. With nine children, I figured that Victoria and Albert must have spent years in this position!)

Artie would laugh, pat my bottom, and say affectionately. "Aaaaaaaawwwwwww, Mama." That didn't help my intestinal fortitude, but it did bolster my ego. There's nothing like togetherness when you're morning-sick.

As soon as the calendar said it was feasible, we went to the family doctor to confirm my accomplished diagnosis. The test tubes agreed and it was unanimous. We had started a baby! As I was leaving the examination room to join Artie in the waiting room, we both flinched when the receptionist shouted at the top of her lungs, "Your maternity charge will be included in the final billing!" There it was— that word. Not "in the family way" not "gravidity confirmed", not even "pregnancy!" No, she yelled out, "Maternity!" Now the whole world (or at least the waiting room) would know what we did! (Done with finesse, I might add.)

As summer passed I learned all the things omitted from the books on 'How to Succeed in Pregnancy Without Really Trying.' For instance, you can't stand as close to anything as you once could—the kitchen sink, the ironing board, or even your husband. Special techniques have to be worked out to compensate such as doing the dishes sideways. Ironing is done without being able to see what you're pressing… or burning.

Most awkward, you have to lean forward while your husband kisses you and holds you up to keep you from falling on your face.

Another problem is keeping the front of the maternity smock clean. It's always six to eight inches ahead of the rest of you. It not only rubs on everything you bend over (*see sink **And ironing board above) but it has a way of catching all those drips and crumbs of food which previously dropped unnoticed from you lips to the napkin on your lap while dining. And forget your lap. It doesn't exist. Neither does the possibility of crossing your legs. During long and boring conversations you can only sit with your legs crossed at the ankles while trying to find a place to cross your arms. They usually end up resting on your ever present shelf, your stomach.

By the end of summer I was fulfilling the definition, "heavy with child." Actually, "obese with child" was more like it. It's just impossible to look sexy when you're seven months pregnant. I know—I tried. Really, I did. In a long, black, nylon nightie, I would stand provocatively in a doorway seeming to lounge against the door jam while "child" hung out in space in the next room. Or there was the demure look over the shoulder as I walked down the hall, full back to Artie. But sooner or later (sooner in our small house) I would reach the end of the hall and have to turn around. There, even in a red lace negligee, I would look

"Sweet," "Like a Madonna," or like a lump! But... definitely not sexy! And by the time you're eight months pregnant, you have to stop trying.

Now, I have an apt footnote on the baby's movement. In the first months, I waited with great anticipation for the first movement. When it came, I didn't shout, "The baby moved!" the way women do in the movies. This expert just thought she had gas! For the next five months there is no doubt about movement. The prenatal infant spends its life kicking mother at every moment. But the child will be perfectly still if anyone, especially the father, puts their hand on the stomach. I don't know how the baby knows, but it will not kick if father's hand is near. For example—

Me: "Here Artie, quick, it's really kicking. Put your hand here."

He: "I can't feel anything."

Me: "Wait, it'll start again."

He: "That's what you said last Sunday when we sat for three hours with my hand on your stomach."

Ten minutes later, after absolute stillness, Artie leaves the house for the store. The baby starts the Can-Can! My baby particularly liked doing the breast stroke. I could feel he or she kick off using my bladder as a spring board, then do the frog kick and bump her or his head on the other side. By the eighth month I knew definitely that the child would grow up to be a boxer by using my right kidney as a punching bag. Had great rhythm and style that child!

As November began, I felt sure that the doctor

had fooled me about the authenticity of my condition. (One thing I've learned about experts—if you think there's a mistake, blame it on another expert.) I was sure that I really had a gigantic tumor. I was just about to swoon into the final scene from *Camille* when sure enough, right during prime T.V. hours, I got a twinge. The twinges turned into twangs. As soon as Jimmy Stewart proved that a man in a body cast can outmaneuver a murderer with flash bulbs, (one couldn't leave in the middle of a Hitchcock movie) I called the doctor and we were on our way.

After eighteen hours of labor during which I slept (notice my efficient use of time?) Artie kept watch. The nurses kept saying, "Aren't you ready yet?" Finally, I was *really* ready considering the labor pains and a magical number of dilation. I waved to Artie as I was gracefully wheeled away into Delivery! Now I'm sure all readers have taken Health IA so I won't go into detailed description of my relative position on the birthing table. My doctor was there and a strange doctor with his mask and costume green scrub pajamas. When no one was looking, the new doctor, seated at my right shoulder, bent down and kissed me! I gave a gasp. "Gasp!"

It was supposed to be a gasp of indignation but then I recognized the new "doctor" to be my own Prince Charming.

"Hark, my dear," he whispered. (I seemed to remember that being the expression which started the whole program.) "Since I was in on the beginning of this project, I thought I'd stay through to the end."

"Charming, you're a prince of a guy!"

The events that followed were in cinemascope, living color, and stereophonic sound. That includes my adroit impression of a Bassett Hound in labor. It was one of those particular, rare moments when the bay of a hound seemed to express my feeling exactly. At one point the doctor interrupted his witty lecture on the events to say, "Artie, breathe!" It seems ol' Artie would hold his breath on each of my contractions, just to help out, and he had forgotten to exhale. After Artie's breathing pattern was better established, we got on to the real business at hand.

Then, there he was. He was all the beauty of a miracle, a fairy tale become reality. At that moment the absurdities of tax deductions were realized. There was now a living personage, our baby. I've yet to find any expert who can describe the true realization of that moment of sharing.

Long Live the King! Hip Hip Hurray!

That was some years ago. I know I became an expert on child rearing. I grew somewhat concerned over the psychological adjustments of an only child. (If I'm going to be an expert, I may as well sound like one.) As a matter of fact, one day when Artie was trudging home, I met him at the door and said, "Hark, my dear..."

Now, I know my "expertise" is a bit outdated. (Okay, I admit, it's very dated.) As I sit in the Family Doctor vestibule waiting for my old lady shots, I see young men and women entering with babies, toddlers, and disgruntled teenagers. Instead of hiding their bellies with voluminous maternity smocks, young women may now wear spandex to emphasize it. Attending men usually carry new infants in a carrier seat that is heavy-duty enough to be thrown out of an airplane with minimum damage to the child. Babies have pacifiers beaded in colors and attached to their clothing so they can sample its comfort on demand. Toddlers play peekaboo with other patients then run back to a parent if startled. Almost all of them, children and parents, are sucking on some liquid in bottle. Teens, who aren't old enough to be referred to older practices, sit disdainfully looking at their phones. Oh, yes, some of the toddlers have phones but I've yet to see a baby with one.

When I see two rough construction men with beards and football shirts, carrying a baby and waiting with the mother, I recognize the special look they give to the little miracle in their charge. The whole drama of pregnancy has many more acts than I experienced with my tadpole swimming Amniotic fluid. The wonder of it all remains.

Maybe now, I'll speak as an expert Grandmother!

Ms. Petra and the Pumpkin

As a newly credentialed Art teacher in the community, Petra was excited by her first teaching position at the middle school but was not really meeting students. Because of COVID distance learning, teaching pods, and teleinstruction, Petra missed the personal interaction with pupils. Art classes were meant to be interactive with the teacher encouraging, the student creating, and the observer appreciating the finished product.

Once schools re-opened full time, Petra could return to the classroom structure she loved. Petra was eager for the school year ahead with her art room established. The excitement diminished when she was shown to her "classroom" on teacher prep day. Instead of desks, there were tables with mismatched chairs. A few racks held various shards and types of paper. A sink looked as if cans of paint had been stored in it. A bulletin board held a partial sign: "Welcome Back" with mispelled graffiti filled in. By the time she had straightened the room, she was exhausted and went to the Teacher's Lounge. There was hardly anybody there. The posted class schedule showed no other art teachers—not even a shop teacher. All creativity funding was designated to the digital labs. She only had one computer in her classroom, and the art software was dismally antiquated. She couldn't see teaching art design in a way meaningful to her students who had better art software at their home computers.

The first days of school were strenuous and Petra wished she could fit in with other faculty. They seemed to be well acquainted with each other, willing to help a new teacher, but very busy with their own classroom setups. Day by day, Petra worked to establish herself in this endeaver but needed some kind of hook to land in the young students who would be in in her charge. Then it came to her! In October, there would be opportunity to join the community "Halloween Drive" celebration.

Decided at the PTA meeting, for a variety of reasons, parents agreed to forgo house-to-house Trick or Treating. Now, post-Covid, parents would chauffer children around the neighborhood in long processions, to see decorations. The youngsters could pop out of the car to pick up packaged, safe candies in front yard bins. They could twirl and dazzle the homeowner on the porch with their costumes, then pop back into the safety of the automobile.

It would be very different from the memory Petra cherished of Halloween. She remembered trudgeing through the darkened night with a pack of school friends. Their homemade costumes were dominated by hoboes and whimsical princesses. The older kids wanted to tour all the way to the school and back and the younger children were eager for the additional treasures. Going up on the porches, the shout "Trick or Treat" would cause the door to open to a person handing out candy, homemade candy apples, and Petra's favorite: popcorn balls. Sometimes their paper bags would tear and they would beg a new grocery sack from their benefactor. (Wiser mothers would give their children pillow cases to hold the wealth.) After hours of gathering treats, Petra would return home exhausted. After a quick snack, exploring her plunder would wait until morning. Then each piece would be evaluated and categorized. Fudge, apples, and popcorn balls were rated highest. Commercial candies and gum put aside for later consumption. Occaisionally a few coins clinked. It was glorious!

Remembering, Petra knew children loved scary pumpkins. She decided to create the greatest pumpkin ever seen in the community to scare shildren and impress the faculty. She would be proud to demonstrate what an art teacher could do! Researching online, Petra found a creatively monstrous design for the upcoming event! Her front yard display of a snarling, undead zombie creature would be terrifying. Oh, yes, a zombie pumpkin would be horrible. Perfect!

Fall colors began changing early and Petra eagerly started collecting accessories, decorations, and plans for her first pumpkin scene in her new neighborhood. She bought a pumpkin shaped tray for treats and lots of verified safe and nutricious snacks. At the grocery store a huge variety of pumpkin gourds were assorted on bales of hay in the parking lot except for one large orange squash sitting by itself. Children picked up and handled the choice smaller pumpkins but seemed to ignore the solitary giant. Petra thought it should be entered in one of those "Biggest Ever" contests. She decided she had to have it although it took two carry-outs to load it in her car. At home, she had to ask the two college guys from down the street to carry it into her kitchen and leave it on the cutting board table.

"How are you going to handle that?" one hefty student asked increduously.

Petra laughed, "Oh, I'll just cut away anything that isn't zombie-like. I have a handy-dandy pumpkin carving set to help." She wiggled the orange utensil case at them, having purchased it online.

The day before Halloween arrived and Petra stroked the smooth orange skin of the giant winter squash. It epitomized the name of Cucurbita Maxima and she knew she must start on her creative venture. Caressing its curves, it was almost sinful to cut through to the ripe flesh below.

Picking up the plastic serrated knife from her Handy Dandy Pumpkin Carving Set, Petra stabbed into the crown near the stem. She intended to cut a circle to remove seeds. The knife slid off the curve, breaking the blade—the skin was impenetrable! In her imagination, the young woman thought she heard a chortle from deep within the gourd on her cutting board. She tried other utensils from the kit but they couldn't begin to penetrate to the rind beneath the skin.

"All, right, you obese vegetable, you can't beat me." Again Petra thought she heard derisive laughter from within pumpkin. Pulling her large kitchen scabbard from the drawer, she confidently stabbed the crown. "A-hah!" she shouted but the sharp blade curved off the pumpkin and sliced through her other hand. Blood sprayed over the cutting board as she dropped the knife with a scream and ran to the bathroom for first aide.

With a whimper, she ran water over the cut wondering if she needed stitches. Instead, she bandaged it with gauze. "Never get mad at a pumpkin!" she admonished her tear streaked face in the bathroom mirror. Sobered by her own expression, she added, "Get even!"

When Petra returned to the kitchen with her bandaged hand, she carried the drill, chisles, and hammer she sometimes used in her art work. She must conquer the pumpkin! How could she ever teach art to a classroom of rowdy middle schoolers if she let an oversized, malevolent pumpkin reduce her to weeping?

Petra started the electric drill and went after the pumpkin but the cord sparked from the outlet. A force from the squash turned the tool back at Petra as she fumbled, not able to control it. Trying to hold the drill away, a touch of panic made her hand tremble. She threw the drill onto the floor now becoming slippery with juice. Breathing harshly, Petra grabbed for her chisel and hammer then gasped. The evil pumpkin created by her imagination, snarled! A foul effigy emerged from beneath her shaking hands.The beast was carving itself! Folds opened, cracks deepened and a hideous face appeared. Shocked by ugliness of the design, Petra tried again to slice the protective skin—to cut away the evil countenance. Tendrils of umber pumpkin flesh slithered out of bulbous eyes. From the toothless grimace of the slash marks where a tongue should have been, only putrid seeds were vomited.

Growling screetches vibrated in the locked stare between the orange zombie and the woman. Screams of a banshee ravaged the room. Were they Petra's or the monstrosity flailing on the cutting board?

In the dark of Halloween night, the children in cars exclaimed when they saw decorations purchased at the local Big Box Store. There was only a dark house where their art teacher lived. Faint lights flickered from inside like candles being extinguished.

J.W. CAPEK

In front of Ms. Petra's house there was a table with a black tablecloth, lots of synthetic spider webs, a battery operated candelabra of flickering LED lights and a tray of hermitically sealed pieces of pumpkin tarts. Each piece included a list of ingredients and warnings about peanuts, nuts, milk products, and gluten. After all, Ms. Petra was a credentialed teacher.

HAVE TO GO BACK

It was the summer, 1950, in Tucson Arizona and they were leaving me! My playmates were leaving me behind so they could go to school!

As the summer was ending, Larry and Sonny and the other guys were more interested in getting ready for school than playing with me. They had deserted me every year for just the same reason, but Mother always told me I was too young, I would have to wait. I would pass the days waiting for their daily return.

Just this past summer, I had grown and grown to catch up and Mother said she thought I was ready for school even if my March birthday would make me wait another year. She also was getting ready for a little brother or sister for me to arrive in the Fall and she had hoped to have me in school by then. I must admit, I probably whined a lot about the guys going away.

Finally, Mother decided it was worth a try—a try

to get me into school so she could have her time when the new baby arrived. The August day we approached our Catholic school became the turning point of my 5 ½ year old life.

The principal of our parish school was named Sister Benedicta. She was at least ten feet tall and wore the full black habit of her Benedictine order. A starched white wimple framed her pale face. The black veil accented her stern expression. Rosary beads were at her waist. She stood next to a massive desk that looked small in comparison. I had grown that summer, but now I shrunk considerably looking up. On the wall above her desk was a crucifix just like the one in church, only smaller. A religious figure was watching us.

"Why is her name different from yours?" I remember her asking.

"Her father was killed in the War just after she was born," Mother explained.

I don't know if Sister's expression softened or hardened. "Then she's a war orphan."

"She's not an orphan! I am her mother, I re-married and soon Janice will have a sibling!" It was always important to Mother that I was *not* an orphan. She had argued with her own mother over the use of the term "orphan."

"She's really too young for this school year. She'll have to wait," Sister said in a serious voice and changed the subject by touching some papers on her desk.

"But Sister, she's as tall as the others in first grade, and I know she's ready. She plays with the older kids on the block, she loves stories and is beginning to read. She really wants to be here," Mother coaxed.

Mother was trying hard, but the ten foot tall nun just shook her head. "This is not a kindergarten, we don't have one. Our first graders have a full day and a full curriculum, and her birthday is too late. She'd be a year younger than her classmates." She sounded final to me, and I started to shrink a little bit more.

"Sister Benedicta, I know Janice is ready and eager for school. Now is the time, she should be in school!" Mother sounded even more final. She was not a person to back down once her mind was set, not even when it meant disagreeing with a school principal in a nun's habit. Sister Benedicta was facing a pregnant woman fighting for her child.

The principal shook her head again making the white wimple stretch a little around her face. She turned to face me fully and looked down at me with an expression I would later wonder about. Was it scrutiny or exasperation?

I stood as tall as I could and looked her right back in the eye. About a hundred years passed for me before the Principal spoke again. She looked directly at me and said, "All right! All right! We'll give her a try. But if she can't keep up, she'll have to go back!"

FACETS of PERCEPTION

Those words were emblazoned on my soul! The Principal of the school had spoken and the figure on the cross heard the proclamation. I know that memories can change, dialogue can adapt, phrases may go astray over time, but the dictum of the grade school principal was never lost. When a ten foot tall nun in a black habit said "If she can't keep up," the gauntlet was thrown down! I would spend a good deal of my life energy being sure I would not have to go back. (Sometimes her words were accompanied by a harsh, gnarled pointed finger. Visual images can be added to traumatic memories over time.)

I had been granted a boon, I was being allowed to attend school. Through grade school, I always "kept up." My above grade average ensured I was where I belonged. Yet, at the end of a school year I was always concerned about passing. "Dear Grandma," I would write. "I sure hope I pass."

By public high school, I was in the top classes, but always looking up to the brilliant students who seemed to naturally understand what the Advanced Placement teachers were teaching. Personally, I had to work harder and instructors seemed to respect that. One math teacher told me, "I could always recognize when I was explaining a new concept well. If I looked at your face, and you were confused, I knew other students would be as well, and I'd adjust my explanation."

When the school year would start every

September, I would have "the nightmare." I would be back in first grade, sometimes naked, always too big for my little desk. As I grew even more, I was more awkward and stuck in the little desk. There was always some authority figure telling me I hadn't worked hard enough. I didn't leave the autumnal bad dream behind and even took it to college. Graduating with a BA in History still meant I needed to keep up to earn a California teaching credential.

Eventually, working towards a Master's degree in education, I started the college semester with the same old dream. This time, I was a fully grown woman with a husband and children and forced to sit in a kindergarten chair. (Of course, I was naked but that had ceased to phase me even though all the small children around me were fully clothed.)

The nightmare began as a faceless professor pointed at me (with a gnarled, bony finger) and declared I would "have to go back!" Finally, I had it! I could be as defiant as needed. I stood up to my full height, kicked aside the baby desk, and spoke directly to the professor with my teacher voice. "You can't make me go back! I have my own teaching credential, my own classroom, and I am a specialist in Learning Disabilities as well as the founder of the Shoestring Technoclassroom Telecommuncations Project!"

That did it! I never had the nightmare again. I never had to "go back." Not to kindergarten, anyway.

FACETS of PERCEPTION

The dream ended there. I didn't go back except in memories, experiences, and events. People became characters living their lives in the facets of my mind.

(As an aside, I am usually fully clothed in my current dreams!)

Author's Note

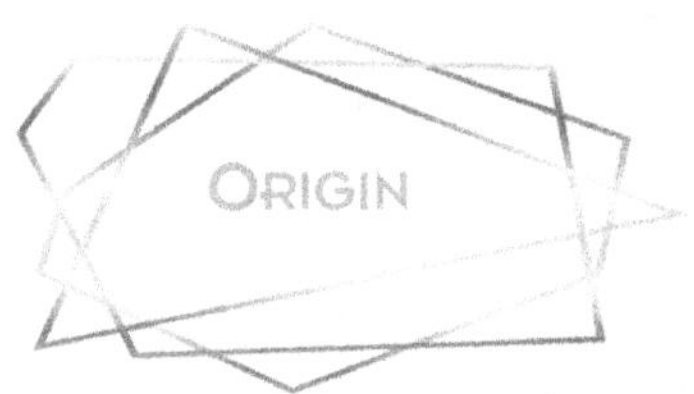

The story began before I was born... and may finally end after I am gone. Already World War II is passing to the stage of myths. It is not often told around campfires or family hearths. Instead, it is re-enacted on video games where a battle can be changed by a reset button, a soldier can die many deaths, and the war enacted from all political sides. It was very real to the generation that lived it... not the sterile, digest war of documentaries but the experience of being alive and part of that special time.

Historians may dissect battles and write biographies. They may draft all the mistakes and misjudgments, all the truths now disclosed, but most of them will never live through such an emotionally charged series of events. Reading is not the same as smothering in a submarine under depth charge attack. Sitting at a computer game is nothing to being in the freezing wind from the bomb bay of a B-17. There is no "reset" button when you are bleeding your life away on a black sand beach.

As for the veterans of World War Two, their families, and the generation now passing, it will be sad if only history books and TV series are left of such a honored and legendary time. Legends continue... they tell a story of something that really happened... or that we wished had happened... or hope will happen.

My father was killed two weeks after I was born. A definitive sentence. For my life, for our family life, for the search of more than 80 years, it was an unequivocal list of words that were always strung together. I was born... my father was killed. It's not as if I had anything to do with it, or even that we knew how or where or even *if* he was killed. No, it was not cause and effect. It was just the way my entry into the family was marked. It helped explain why my name was different from the rest of the family. It identified the portrait of the handsome young Army aviator that hung in our home. It kept alive a mystery story that began on March 31, 1945... just two weeks after I was born...

MARRIAGE FUGUE

Hello, Mr. Hargrove, come on in and have a seat. I'm Peter Hall, Marriage Counsellor," said the tall, red haired man with a big smile.

I didn't say anything. I was only here as a last resort. We shook hands and he went on talking as if I couldn't read his title on the door.

"As you know, Mr. Hargrove, I have been talking with your wife and I have heard her side of the story. I have to say up front, your marriage does appear... *troubled*. Today, it's your turn to tell your story. Once you tell me your side, we'll get you two together as a couple and see if we can improve things for you."

I sat in the chair to which Dr. Hall directed me. I looked around the comfortable, inviting office and noted the professional atmosphere. I decided to go along with this marriage counsellor. I doubted counseling would work, but it wouldn't hurt to try. I was ready to try almost anything, even divorce.

"Now, Keith. Is it okay if I call you Keith? Please call me Peter. It's been my experience that things go more smoothly if we talk on an informal basis. Now, first off, how do you think your wife described your marital situation?" said Peter.

"Oh, I don't know, I just have a hard time talking about intimate stuff like this." He wanted to talk, I didn't.

"That's okay. It's quite common to be reluctant. Relax and take a few deep breaths, close your eyes, if you wish. Just tell me what you think your wife's problem is with your marriage.

I took a breath but the tension remained. "Well, my guess is she said I'm careless, dull, and didactic. I am a lawyer with a firm in the city and am away from home quite a bit. At least it is convenient, we both have our work. A little bit better than being single. She probably added that our life together is boring, she's made that quite clear to me—over and over again... and our sex life is perfunctory, at best." I was generous with that description of our non-existing intimacy.

Peter pursed his lips and wrote some notes in his notebook. "That's quite a summation. Hmm... That's strange..." said Peter, "Those were almost her exact words. Tell me, what do you think is the main problem in your marriage?"

"Simple. She definitely has an attitude of superiority and contempt for those she considers to be inferior, which means mostly me. Nothing I do seems to satisfy her anymore. She resents my time working. What's the point in trying?"

"Keith is there anything you two actually enjoy doing together?" asked Peter.

"We watch TV together, we still have cable. Sometimes we stream newer movies. It's okay. Even then, we rarely watch the same things. We used to like music a lot, but that seems to have faded away."

"Why do you suppose the music lost its appeal?" Peter asked.

I was getting tired of Peter's questions but his change of subject was intriguing.

"Oh, we were young, it was rock, classic rock, which is mostly out of favor today. What is popular today just isn't any good for Gwen and me,"

"You and Gwen really liked classic rock, didn't you? Perhaps it was early in your relationship?"

I fidgeted, remembering the dances we used to attend. I nodded.

"Keith, you may feel you are boring and didactic, but I think we can work through this. It will take some time and you will have to open your mind and give up many of your preconceived ideas." Peter went on, "Gwen was pretty sure you would be resistant to anything I would suggest. Was she right?"

He trapped me! Gwen had put him up to this. She was teaching me a lesson.

After a long pause I said, "No. I'm willing to give

anything a try. Within reason. I guess I've nothing to lose." *My life is so uneventful and boring I am willing to do almost anything.*

Peter decided to make a jump in their efforts, "Keith, you need to open yourself to a wider range of music. I want you to consider some different music."

"A wider range of music? Why? What are you, a marriage counselor or a disc jockey? What good ever came from music? Most of it is a waste of time," I said with a voice a little higher than it need be.

Peter said, "Lately, you've only been exposed to the crass, tinny music right? That's not real music, not deep, harmonious music, and certainly not beautiful music."

"I see no real content in or purpose for music, anymore!" I responded. "I'm only here because—"

Peter came right back with, "Now you are being obstinate and inflexible, in addition to boring and didactic. Spoken just like a boring lawyer." His grin softened the words.

My hackles went up. I resented any anti-lawyer comments. *You pompous jerk. You have no reason to talk to me that way,* I thought to myself. When I looked at Peter, who was smiling, I realized, *He's just trying to get a rise out of me!*

At following sessions, I thought we wasted a great deal of time arguing about the value of music. Peter said to me, "You don't comprehend the structure of a good classical musical composition, do you?"

I responded, "What's any of this have to do with marriage counseling?"

Peter suddenly blurted out, "Rhythm, rhyme, harmony."

"What are you talking about?" I replied. "Seriously, I have other things to do."

Peter said, "Rhythm, rhyme, and harmony comprise the essence of music. You might know the definitions of those three words, but you are not paying attention to the depth of their meaning. Rhythm is more than the beat of music; it is the heart which pumps melody and harmony through any musical work. "Fast, slow, weak, strong, regular, irregular it doesn't matter. Beat is at the core, the heart. It can also be said of a husband and wife."

"Next, rhyme is a control function which applies repeating patterns to music which make it smoother, more enjoyable, and more easily remembered. Think of the patterns you and Gwen have shared over your marriage."

"Finally, comes harmony, which adds the depth of chords to the work, simultaneous multiple notes which bring richness and nuance."

Why was he going on like this about classical music? I came here for marriage counseling, not lessons in classical music. Why is Peter so determined I should understand music the way he does?

"Doesn't marriage have all three?" Peter asked quietly.

Finally, I gave in and said, "Okay. I agree to try music your way, but I'm not expecting much from it."

Peter replied, "At least try to keep an open mind. We'll start you off with Vivaldi: Concerto in D Major, 2nd movement for guitar and violins. Keep rhythm, rhyme, harmony in mind while you listen to it. Will you do that for me?"

"Yeah," I sighed, hoping this would end the session..

Peter gestured to the couch and told me to relax while he set up the music. He set up his stereo and put on a record. I was surprised that it was an old vinyl LP but listened as Peter requested.

The music was... well, it was music. It was okay, but nothing spectacular. When the piece was finished I remarked, "So what? The music was familiar, it's just background for movies, isn't it? That does nothing for me."

Peter suggested, "Listen carefully and take note of the vibrations produced by the guitar and violins, and observe the subtleties the musicians created by the speed at which the guitar was plucked and the bows were drawn over the strings. People can immerse themselves in this music and actually experience a physical thrill, which many describe as spine tingling or chilling."

Peter played the piece again.

"Nothing happens for me. What is supposed to happen? Maybe my brain does not operate the way yours does," I said although I would admit listening made a restful interlude.

Peter replied, "It might take time to appreciate the beauty of music. Time to appreciate a relationship. You should browse the music archives and listen to different types of music. Not all people react the same way to the many styles of music. Talk to Gwen about it."

I listened to all sorts of music but never felt anything from it other than a slightly relaxed sensation, certainly nothing like a thrill. Peter said people in remote small villages created their own music using primitive instruments. I listened to some of the music from primitive groups, but found the music to be discomforting in an oddly eerie sort of way.

With that, Peter said, "You're making progress! You are decerning your preferences."

Making progress? A lawyer made ill at ease by people playing flutes and beating on drums was progress? How was this going to help? I was beginning to question Peter's veracity, but, at least there some emotion connected with music. At home, Gwen would come into my office and sit with me while the music was playing.

I was ready to cancel future appointments and the music when Peter finally asked me why. I could not really explain. I said, "I just see no point in going on with music study. I get nothing from it."

Peter asked, "Have you shared any music with Gwen?"

"She listens sometimes but we don't really talk about it."

Peter replied, "You really should try that. I'm certain she will react differently than you have. Give it a try. You've got nothing to lose."

"Peter, I do not think playing music to Gwen at this point would do any good." *Why should I give Gwen an opportunity to criticize and belittle me for my lack of music appreciation? I had failed to comprehend music in any basic way and I just did not want any ridicule from Gwen about it.*

Peter said, "Let me suggest you try my suggestion. I recommended Antonio Vivaldi's Concerto in D Major. Try it again. It's a classical piece and it may let you get deeper into the music. Keith, remember something—classical music has been driving lovers nuts and making them cry for a couple hundred years. Give it a chance.

"People crying over a bit of music? That is not possible," I replied.

"It happens. Take my word for it," said Peter.

"Yeah, well, I just don't see it working," I said, "But I'll give it a try."

As I was leaving Peter added one more thing, "Keith, play Vivaldi when you and Gwen make love."

"What? Are you nuts? Why would I do that?" I was almost shouting at him.

"Just try it Keith. You may be surprised. Promise you'll try it." said Peter.

"Okay, okay, okay," I said, mainly to make Peter shut up.

I went to a music store specializing in classical stuff and found Vivaldi's Concerto in D Major, plus another Vivaldi set called The Four Seasons. Peter had told me to open myself to the music, to let it flow into me and through me. He reminded me to appreciate the orchestral texture provided by the mix of instruments which played the very intricate and delicate music score of this particular symphony. Peter had added I should constantly remain aware of the tempo at which the delicate notes were played. I wondered what that had to do with appreciating the music. He must be making all this up as he went along. *What did it have to do with our marriage problems?*

I followed Peter's instructions and the reward was remarkable. The music was beautiful and I did experience emotion. I was stunned. I wanted to tell Gwen about this. I needed her to join me in tasting this wonderful new pleasure.

"Gwen, do you and Peter spend most of the session talking about music?" I asked one morning as we passed in the hall. Both of us were preparing for our separate work.

She paused to look at me. "Part of it, I'm learning new things. You and I seemed more musically inclined when we were first married." She answered my direct question with a slight smile.

"First married... seems long ago."

Gwen's expression tightened, "At least you're going to sessions, you admit we need help."

"Because I am careless, boring, and didactic?" I quoted her sarcastically. That ended the moment. Later, while reviewing cases, I thought of her and remembered the morning. Especially her expression. On a whim, I called a booking agent for information on concerts in the city.

In the evening, Gwen finished her chores and sat next to me on the couch in the living room. "I have papers to correct... Did Peter suggest this?" she asked, hearing the music. "He's suggested I should listen to it... with you." The television wasn't mentioned.

I said, "We need to listen to some music together, as a couple. It is very important for both of us... according to Peter."

Gwen and I listened to Vivaldi with low lighting, appliances turned off. We sincerely *listened*. I realized she had been receiving the same therapy as I. We exchanged opinions about the structure of the symphony and the beauty of each passage. We experienced emotions never before felt as the various instruments in the orchestra each contributed their unique, beautiful parts to the body of music. We actually had fun doing it. We were *talking about something new.*

In the past, I had considered much of the music to which I listened to be muddy and confused, but in sharing Vivaldi with Gwen and experiencing it together, a clarity descended upon both of us and new exciting feelings bubbled up in us to be savored and enjoyed. At the end of the evening we touched hands and went to our separate bedrooms.

The next evening, we tried the other Vivaldi, The Four Seasons, which was longer. The tempo variations of the music was agonizing at times.

I hate to admit this, tears actually came to my eyes. Gwen cried too, and she added, "The instruments are crying, each in their own unique way."

I had not thought of it that way, but she was right. The violins were weeping, and soon, so were we. We moved next to each other on the sofa and I put my arms around Gwen.

As the Four Seasons played we would sink into deep despair only to be pulled up in joyous flight. At some points time almost ceased its movement and we hung there in anticipation of what would come next to take us to another thrilling experience. Simultaneously, we realized we were holding each other tightly.

We began pulling each other's clothing off and began making love as we never had before. Never had I seen my lovely wife cry as we made love, but Vivaldi made it happen.

We lingered there, suspended, hoping it would never end. Yet, at the same time, wishing it would, because we were not sure we could endure any more of the exquisite beauty we were experiencing. How could humans have ever created such beauty? How could we have overlooked it?

It did finally end with an exhilarating crescendo. Gwen and I were suspended in some other place where time did not move and we, together, were simultaneously immersed in total joy. Our tears mingled, together, finally a couple again, we achieved full understanding of the term *"spine tingling."*

As the music ended, a contentment engulfed us and held us together in an unimagined closeness. It provided warmth and comfort such as neither of us had ever imagined or realized we needed. Exhausted, we drifted off to sleep, holding each other closely, knowing our marriage had been set right.

We went together to Peter's office to discuss our success. He was delighted at our progress. Gwen and I told him the music to which he had introduced us was magic. Together, we told him our marriage had been on the cusp of failure before we came to him.

Peter smiled as he exclaimed, "I love it when it turns out like this!"

I asked him, "How did you come up with classical music as therapy for failing marriages?"

Peter paused then made a decision. "I was an orphan and raised by the village of Winsome. You may have passed it sometime. Growing up, I loved music but also wanted to take care of others the way people took care of me. Winsome sponsored me through college where I was able to find the way to do both. And, here I am." He stroked his red hair as he completed the thought.

His answer surprised Gwen and me. "It's not always classical music," the counsellor continued. That depends on the couple. I just talk to a couple, then I make a judgement about the best music for them. It's all about the rhythm, rhyme, harmony which best suits a particular couple. For you two classical seemed the best fit. Other types of music might work as long as it is slow music. That's your key.

As Peter ushered us from his office he said, "The Romans had a saying, *Festina lente*, it means 'make haste slowly' which sounds illogical, but if you think about it, the same should be said of love, and love should be accompanied by music—exhilarating music, which, if played properly and timed for just the right moment, it will end in a crescendo guaranteed to bring lovers to tears of joy. Now you know the secret. Don't forget it! We'll talk next session."

"Thank you, Peter, but we're taking some time off next week... call it a long date night," I said with a smile to my wife.

Gwen shared my expression and added, "Keith has a collection of concerts we are attending in the city next week. We are going to *enjoy* each one."

"Why don't you two stop at a music store on the way? Treat yourselves. You'll appreciate *The Bolero* by Ravel," Peter suggested, knowingly. "It gives new meaning to Crescendo and Fortississimo!"

PETER AND SCARLET

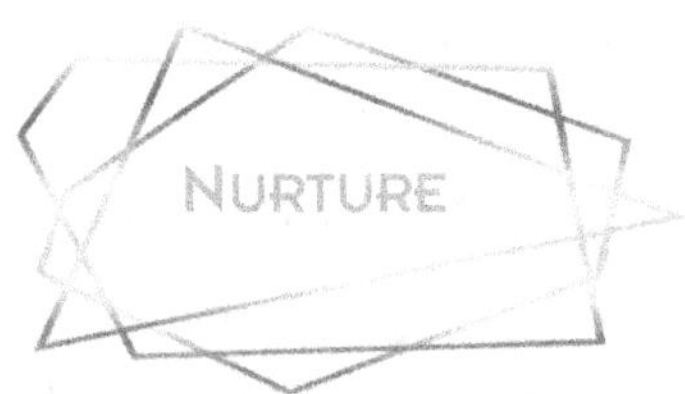

Peter was cutting firewood behind the woodshed when he resolved to do something about himself and Scarlet, his little sister. Tears were pouring from his eyes. Momma had died that morning giving birth to a stillborn baby girl. Peter had watched the birth of the dead baby and had seen his mother's hemorrhaging. He didn't know what to do or how to help. Peter was eight years old.

When momma began the painful birthing, daddy disappeared. Hearing momma's screams, little Scarlet ran and hid in the woodshed, her favorite place. Scarlet was five years old.

Peter realized momma had died and so had the new baby. He covered them there in the bed with momma's favorite quilt.

Daddy came home several hours later. He was drunk, which Peter expected. Daddy pulled the quilt off momma and saw the dead baby. Cursing, he pulled momma from the bed and carried her body outside and put her in the back of his truck then drove away. He left the dead baby on the floor where she had fallen. When their father came back he began to drink. Both the children knew from experience things would get worse.

Peter spoke quietly to Scarlet, "Go get a pillowcase and put your clothes in it. Don't forget your underpants and socks. Bring your coat, it might get cold again and we're getting out of here."

The children left their father alone in the front room of the small house and began moving quietly about the place collecting things they would need. After a few minutes, Peter came into Scarlet's little room and said, "Come on Scarlet, hurry. Daddy's getting worse."

Scarlet said, "What about the baby? Shouldn't we do something with her?"

"Yes," answered Peter. "I plan to take her with us and bury her in the woods, someplace nice where Daddy can't find her."

"My little baby sister…" said Scarlet, as she began to cry.

"Don't start crying now, Scarlet. We'll have to do that later, after we get away," said Peter, with tears welling in his own eyes. "Come on, let's go now."

Peter led the way into the front room. Their father was seated in his favorite chair with his head leaning to one side. He appeared unconscious. Peter motioned Scarlet for her to go to the front door. Peter put his sack of clothing and canned food on the floor next to the baby. Silently, he knelt and gathered the baby and his sack of possessions into his arms. Scarlet opened the door and the two moved outside. Peter stepped off the porch and turning, said to Scarlet, "Let's run, Sister, we have to get away from here."

The Hall children ran farther than they had ever run in their lives. They ran until Scarlet collapsed. Peter turned and said, "Get up Scarlet. I can't carry you, too."

Sensing the fear in her brother's voice, Scarlet got to her feet, grabbed her sack and began to run again.

Finally, Peter stopped running.

"This is far enough for now," said Peter breathing heavily. "This is a good place. I've been here before."

Peter dropped his bundle, then kneeling with great gentleness, he laid the dead infant on the ground. Peter fell over on his back exhausted and went to sleep.

Scarlet sat next to her dead sister and cried for a while before she began to look around. There was a small stream running nearby. Scarlet got up and walked to the little creek, where she washed her hands and face. She went to her bag of clothing and pulled out an old washcloth. She took the cloth to the stream and rinsed it, then she walked to where her sister lay and began to bathe the naked dead baby.

Peter awakened and he began to assist Scarlet in bathing their sister. When they finished, Peter pulled a clean white shirt from his bag and said to Scarlet, "We can wrap her in this."

The pair took the tiny body to the base of a large sycamore tree and scraped a hole with sticks and their hands large enough to hold the body. They wrapped her in Peter' shirt, covered her with dirt, then they searched for rocks to put atop the grave for protection.

"She doesn't even have a name," said Scarlet, beginning to whimper.

"Let's call her Annie. That was momma's name," murmured Peter.

As they covered the baby with the rocks, Peter added, "She's the lucky one."

Two nights later, as the children huddled together for warmth, a large grayish dog came into their little campsite. Peter was sleeping and Scarlet lying next to him froze in terror at the sight of the dog. The animal watched the children for several minutes, then it approached Scarlet and lay beside her to keep her warm. Scarlet soon fell asleep comforted by the huge creature.

The next morning Peter was startled by the large dog when he awoke. He quietly awakened Scarlet and tried to pull her away for the animal for safety.

"No," Scarlet murmured, "She made me warm all night."

Peter began gathering their things, while avoiding the huge dog. He opened their last can of food and gave some to Scarlet. He offered a bit to the dog, but it wouldn't eat. It just stayed close to Scarlet. When the food was gone and they had gathered all their belongings, Peter said, "We have to get moving, Scarlet."

Scarlet said, "I want the dog to come with us. It loves me."

"I don't think so, Sister. We can't feed it," he said. "Anyway, it probably belongs to somebody."

"No, she's my dog now," said Scarlet. "Look at her eyes. They're blue, like mine. She's my Baby Blue Eyes. She loves me and keeps me warm, like Momma did."

Peter gave in, like he always did for Scarlet. Why couldn't she have something she liked?

Days later, the Hall children and Baby Blue Eyes stumbled into village of Winsome, seemingly by accident. The first person they encountered was Lewis Franklin, at that time a man nearing middle age, a lifelong resident and the honorary mayor of Winsome. Lewis saw them walking along the highway, so he crossed the street and walked up to the group.

"Are you kids lost?" said the man.

Neither of the two spoke up immediately.

Lewis saw they were afraid and said, "Don't worry. You're in Winsome. Nobody will hurt you here. You look tired and hungry. Would you like something to eat?"

"Yeah, we ain't had no eats in two days," said the

little girl.

"Shut up, Scarlet! He'll call the sheriff," whispered the boy.

"No, don't worry. I won't call the law. In fact, we don't even have a sheriff here in Winsome. You kids and your dog just walk along with me up to Peggy's Place. The diner is up the road. You can see it right up there at the intersection," he said, pointing up the road to his right. "We'll get you two and the Weimaraner filled up with some good grub real soon."

"That's Baby Blue Eyes. My dog," said Scarlet.

"And a beautiful dog she is," said Mr. Franklin.

In five minutes the trio were entering Peggy's Place. The man held the door for the children, and spoke in quietly to the waitress, "Clair, I found you a pair of hungry redheads out on the highway."

"Hungry redheads. Huh? Well kids, if you're hungry, we'll find something to fill you up," said the server with a big smile. "Come on over to this first booth and take a load off. I'll start you off with a couple of glasses of nice, cold milk. Okay?"

"Yeah," said the boy, almost crying, with his voice quivering. "M... milk sounds real good."

Clair returned in a few moments with two large glasses of milk and set them in front of the children.

The man spoke up, "If you kids really haven't eaten in days, don't drink that milk too fast. Just take it slow. Okay?" He turned to Clair and said, "Let's have two kid-sized meals with scrambled eggs, sausage and a short stack of pancakes. Okay?"

"Yes sir," Clair replied.

The sisters, Peggy and Clair, still young women, lived together in a large old house they had inherited from their parents. Neither was married, or otherwise engaged at that time, so they decided, at Mr. Franklin's urging, to take the Hall children into their home and give them a safe place to live until it was decided where they belonged. No one ever searched for them, no one claimed them missing. Having found a haven, the Hall children never left Winsome. Winsome never failed them.

When Scarlet arrived in Winsome she was only five years old, and they had been a hard five years. Initially, the only person she trusted was her brother, but with the passage of time she came to care for Winsome and all of its unusual residents. Scarlet had never known an adult who treated her well, except for her mother and she was now gone. In a short span of time Scarlet's new adult acquaintances had jumped to three. She quickly adjusted to Peggy and Clair because they were so thoughtful of her and reminded her of her mother, but Scarlet didn't know what to make of Mr. Franklin. He was kind, but scary all the same.

Mr. Franklin carried a small black book, which he wrote in once in a while. Scarlet was curious and asked him about it.

"What're all those marks you put in that book?"

"That's writing. Those marks make words," Mr. Franklin replied.

"Why do you do that?" Scarlet inquired.

"These words are notes I make to myself so I won't forget things."

"Can't you just remember stuff?" Scarlet asked.

Mr. Franklin chuckled gently and said, "Oh, Honey, I'm getting older, and old people's heads are full of so much stuff they can't always remember important things. That's why I write them down."

"What if I need to remember something?" said the girl. "I don't know how to write. Peter can write, but I can't."

"Oh, you sweet little girl! You just gave me an idea. We need a school," Lewis exclaimed as he opened his little book and began making notes. Winsome had no official school, so the young children, and others of the town were taught various skills as needed by knowledgeable residents of the town. There was no curriculum, no schoolhouse, nothing formal, but things just seemed to work out and get taken care of as needed. Older students rode a bus to a larger distant town.

Based on their background, Lewis Franklin realized the Hall children required more formal educating in certain areas. He couldn't just ask various citizens to take the children under their wing and teach them reading, writing, history, mathematics, whatever. Something was missing. Lewis puzzled over what would be needed to properly educate Winsome's citizens.

But where do we start? Lewis continued to think on the problem. One day as Lewis was sitting in Peggy's Place, while Clair was making certain he never lacked for fresh, hot coffee, an idea popped: *We can put a classroom in the library!* The magic of Winsome had already provided an old barracks for a building. Kent State had provided the perfect Librarian in Mis Annabel Lee.

The magic of Winsome never failed to amaze Lewis Franklin. Immediately, he set about acquiring the necessities for a classroom in the library for Winsome and the Hall children.

The Winsome Library did work out quite well. The first thing Winsome residents saw upon entering the building was a spectacular wooden desk, which young John Straightarrow had built and intricately carved for the purpose. John added a hand-carved nameplate which sat on the desk and said *Annabel Lee - Librarian.* The residents of Winsome took great pride in their library and their lovely librarian.

Many of the residents of Winsome donated personal books and collections to the new library. Mr. Franklin had donated his Encyclopedia Britannica and Oxford English Dictionary. Annabel Lee put her personal copy of Webster's New Collegiate Dictionary on the shelf and others gave an American Heritage Dictionary of the

English Language, Roget's International Thesaurus, and someone even donated a copy of the US Navy's Blue Jackets Manual, dated 1944. Several private collections of fiction were also donated.

Mr. Franklin was able to obtain copies of the Stone County Recorder's books, and Stone County Sentinel files. The Sentinel was the old newspaper, which was published from the early 1800s until it went bankrupt during the Great Depression.

Once the library was equipped with the necessary furniture and shelving, several residents assisted Miss Annabel Lee in organizing everything. When everything was ready, Mr. Franklin organized a grand opening. Everyone in Winsome agreed the new Library was a splendid place and it became the Pride of Winsome.

Time passed, and Miss Annabel Lee had turned out to be everything Winsome needed for a librarian. She was bright, thoughtful, very well organized, and a splendid planner. Now, all Mr. Franklin had to do was convince Miss Annabel Lee that she should shoulder the task of being Winsome's school teacher, as well as librarian. He began by taking the Hall children to the library and introducing them to Miss Annabel Lee.

Mr. Franklin joined the Hall children for breakfast at Peggy's Place. He figured he would begin by introducing them to the idea of starting formal schooling.

"I know Scarlet has never attended school, but

how about you, Peter? Have you been to school?" the old man began.

"Yes, sir. I finished third grade," Peter said with pride, then continued, "That was plenty for me."

"Third grade, huh. Well, it's a start, but you've a ways to go," Mr. Franklin replied.

"A ways to go? No! I had enough," Peter replied, "It wasn't much fun and there's nothing else for me to learn."

"Oh, Peter. There's a lot more for you to learn. And you, too, Scarlet. You both need to go to school," said Mr. Franklin.

"Why? How much schooling have you had Mr. Franklin?" asked Peter thinking this would somehow put Mr. Franklin on the spot where he would admit Peter needed no more education.

"Well... Let's see. Twelve years of regular public school," he paused a moment, then finished, "and six years of college. That's about it. So, eighteen years total."

"Eighteen years! No! Nobody could stand that much!" Peter was incredulous. "That just can't be right. I'm sorry, Mr. Franklin. I'm not calling you a liar, or nothing, but eighteen years of school would kill a person."

At that moment, Clair came to their booth and topped off Mr. Franklin's coffee. Mr. Franklin said to her, "Clair, how many years of school have you had?"

"I went to school for twelve years, thirteen if you count kindergarten," was Clair's response.

Mr. Franklin raised his voice and called to Peggy, who was working the grill, "How about you, Peggy? How much schooling?"

"Same as Clair. Thirteen counting kindergarten," she called back.

Peter looked like a deer in the headlights. He was caught. Even his little sister realized it.

"You're gonna have to go to school, Peter," she snickered.

"Just shut up, Scarlet. You'll have to go, too. Even longer than I will," said the now-depressed Peter.

"Come on kids. Finish up your breakfast and let's walk down to the library," said Mr. Franklin.

After breakfast, Mr. Franklin escorted Peter and Scarlet down to the Winsome Library where he introduced them to Miss Annabel Lee and the first happy time of their lives began.

Scarlet and Peter prospered in Winsome. In Peggy and Clair's and with Miss Annabel Lee's tutelage they had a place to learn and learn they did. Once the story of the children spread throughout Winsome, the entire population of the town displayed interest in their education. Everyone in the town did their best to help the children along on their journey.

Peter Hall discovered music in the library with a donated collection of classical music, which he studied intensely. Peter happily studied all the subjects Miss Annabel Lee assigned because he was totally captivated by the lovely woman, but music became his obsession.

The music collection, and a beautifully restored Garrard turntable from the 1960's mounted on a handmade walnut plinth on which to play the records, were parts of the music treasure donated by Farley Folkman. Miss Annabel Lee said music emanating from this device was pure and perfect, but the music had an even more profound effect on Peter—the music touched his soul.

Farley, a childless widower, had decided to share the music with everybody in Winsome when Lewis Franklin asked for donations to the library. When he was told of Peter's love for music, Farley volunteered to help Peter in his music studies. Farley spent hours instructing Peter and advising him to study and feel the rhythm, rhyme, and harmony built into music.

At first, young Peter wanted to be a musician and play with a band. Becoming a composer followed, and by high school graduation, Peter's goal was to be a music teacher. Reflecting on the people who helped him and Scarlet, he was torn between the music and psychological studies. Peter wanted to return the kindness and support he had received as a frightened child.

When Farley saw the conflict in Peter, he told him, "Peter, there's no reason you can't do both. You have always been compassionate in taking care of your sister and others. You can help people and share music. It sounds like a Winsome way of life. Continue your studies and you will be able help others." It was Farley who gave Peter a scholarship to study at Kent State.

Scarlet acquiesced to education but lacked the eagerness of her brother. With the passing years she learned to read, she had sufficient vocabulary and grammar to author a decent paper. She was quite good at mathematics. Miss Annabel Lee felt Scarlet had a sense of business acumen but had no idea how to focus that skill.

Something was missing. Now well-educated and a graduate, Scarlet lacked the spark that would ignite her life. She seemed to live from day to day without some vital element which makes life worth living. Miss Annabel Lee discussed the Hall children frequently with Lewis Franklin and one day during such a discussion Mr. Franklin had an idea.

"I've been thinking about the campground. It's nothing more than an open field right now, but what if we built some cabins up there for visitors to Winsome."

"Sounds like a good idea," said Miss Annabel Lee, "But what's it got to do with Scarlet?"

"There's a carpenter here in Winsome. He's a young man, been here awhile. His name is John Straightarrow and he has good recommendations from his tribal leaders. He's the guy who made your desk and nameplate back when you started at the library. He was just a kid then," said Mr. Franklin. "I've been talking with John regarding the building of some rental cabins for visitors, and he's amenable to the idea of building them for us. Couldn't Scarlet be the bookkeeper and business manager for such a project?"

"Oh, yes!" said the librarian. "Scarlet certainly has the perspicacity to handle a job like that. She'll like it. Good idea."

Scarlet finished school but had no desire to leave to go to college when she was asked to come to the library for a meeting with Lewis Franklin and Miss Annabel Lee. She felt trepidation at being asked to appear before the two adults who, more than anyone else in her life, represented authority and responsibility to Scarlet. *Have I done something wrong? Is there a problem? What could it be?*

As Scarlet walked into the library she glanced at the two adults and saw their smiles and was instantly relieved. *This looks okay...*

"Hello, Scarlet," said Mr. Franklin. "Have a seat," he gestured to a chair at the table opposite the two of them.

As Scarlet settled into her chair Mr. Franklin said, "My Dear, Ms. Lee and I have a proposition for you. How would you like a job?"

A job?! ...I never dreamed.... Scarlet's mind raced. "What?"

"Let us explain," said Miss Annabel Lee. "Mr. Franklin and I have been discussing a project for Winsome and we would like you to be a part of it. Would you like to hear the details?"

"Oh, yes," Scarlet said enticed by the idea of a job. "Please tell me."

"For some time," Mr. Franklin began, "we've realized visitors need someplace to stay while visiting Winsome. The old campground just isn't suitable for many people. So, we're planning to build some rental cabins on the campground. Miss Annabel Lee suggested you for bookkeeper and manager for the building project. Would you be interested in a job like that?"

"Oh gosh, yes! I'd love a job like that," Scarlet's previous fears evaporated into joy as she jumped up and ran to hug Mr. Franklin, then Miss Annable Lee.

Scarlet began jumping up and down while crying with joy and repeatedly saying, "Thank you! Thank you! Thank you! Thank you!"

Miss Annabel Lee and Mr. Franklin looked at each other and then, with a big smile, Mr. Franklin said, "That went well."

John Straightarrow, the carpenter, had wandered into Winsome as a teenager. He never spoke of where he was from or if he had family. He seldom smiled other than when he talked about wood and the fashioning of wooden objects and structures. He was a quiet man fond of saying, "A tree died to make this wood. The least I can do is sculpt the wood to reveal the inner beauty that tree possessed." That was John's mantra.

John agreed to do the carpentry for the cabin project. His first cabin was an odd round structure resembling a yurt, except that it was built of wood rather than fabric. The roof was also of wood and it was intricately arched, woven and enfolded to shed water, yet it had no fasteners or nails. No one could tell exactly how John had done it. The finished cabin gave the illusion of being much larger on the inside than it appeared from the outside.

Over the course of a year, John built a small cluster of a dozen cabins on the Winsome campgrounds. All were made of wood. They seemed to need no fasteners of any kind to hold them together, and every one of them was waterproof. They all were of different design and each seemed larger on the inside than they appeared from outside. Each cabin had a complete bathroom and laundry facility. No one in Winsome had any idea of how John had done it.

Scarlet had managed the bookwork for the project and had used less of the funding Winsome had provided for It. The only explanation for the cost savings was that the cabins appeared smaller than planned. Inexplicably, the total interior square footage of the twelve cabins was exactly what the project plans called for.

When Scarlet returned the unused portion of the

cabin funding, Miss Annabel Lee asked how she and John had managed to cut the cost. Scarlet simply said, "John Straightarrow works miracles. He's special."

During the course of the year they spent together building the cabins, Scarlet was able to relax a bit around John Straightarrow. John was a gentle person, which Scarlet came to realize and she let some of the grief and fear she carried fall away when she was with him. Scarlet's behavior aroused sympathy, compassion, empathy in John. It took several months, but John finally realized he was in love with Scarlet.

John was nonplussed by the realization of his love for Scarlet. While Scarlet had let down her guard a bit, she was nowhere near reciprocating the feelings John felt for her. What could he do? The love within him was a fire it seemed he could neither release nor contain.

Finally, John went to speak with Scarlet's brother, Peter, but he stumbled in that attempt, as well. All he could muster when talking to Peter was a question about where to buy music for a woman. It seemed John was doomed to suffer his love for Scarlet in silence.

"Let's check out a few songs first at the library." The two men went directly to the DVD section and Peter quickly pulled a disc. He slipped the disc into a player and a beautiful song began to play.

"That song that's playing? What is it?" asked John.

"It's *Scarborough Fair*," Peter answered, smiling. "It's playing just for you."

"Yeah, that's it, from Simon and Garfunkel's Concert in Central Park, but it sounds different. There's no words," said John, mesmerized by the music.

"This is a different version," said Peter. "It's an instrumental version by a different artist. It's played slowly, very romantically. The song is actually based on two old English folk songs. There are many beautiful interpretations of the piece, but Simon and Garfunkel deserve credit for reawakening the piece for modern audiences."

John was able to do one thing for Scarlet which gained him her everlasting gratitude. He gave her a dog. Scarlet had arrived in Winsome with a devoted older dog. His gradual death was devastating. She never had another dog nor told anyone how her Baby had kept her warm on the frightful night of the runaway. John realized Scarlet was afraid of so many things in life, many of which were specters from her past. John reckoned Scarlet needed a constant companion and guardian, so he began the search for the best dog he could find for that purpose.

There was a new veterinarian in Winsome, Blaine Guthrie, DVM. John marched himself down to the vet's office and asked him for advice about a dog. John explained that he needed a good guardian for a friend of his, without mentioning her name. He told the vet about the woman's childhood and the difficult life she had.

Dr. Guthrie was a gentle man with a warm smile.

He only asked John one question, "Would this lady be fearful of a big dog?"

"No, I don't think so," was John's reply. "She's never been afraid of any animals. Just people."

"I understand. Well, in that case, she would be best off with maybe a yellow Labrador, or better yet, a Weimaraner."

"Weimaraner?" John questioned. "Would one of them really be okay for her?"

"Oh, yes! Absolutely!" said the doc. "Weimaraners are a breed that will be a friendly but fearless companion. Excellent for the situation you've described."

John set about searching for a Weimaraner puppy. It took him a few weeks, but he found someone in a town several miles from Winsome had posted an ad offering Weimaraner puppies. The man who responded to John's phone call told him there was only one puppy left, so he should come right over to see it.

When he arrived at the house John was greeted by an older couple. He explained he was looking for a Weimaraner because a vet had recommended the breed.

The old woman reached down and picked up the lone puppy in the kennel. As she turned to hand the puppy to John, the puppy looked at him. The dog had piercing blue eyes.

Startled, John stepped back and said, "Wow, those eyes! Is that normal?"

"Sure, blue eyes occur commonly in Weimaraners,

and a few other breeds, too," said the old man.

"That's impressive," said John, "but will the eyes stay that color?"

"Oh, yes. They certainly will," the couple said in unison.

Reaching for his wallet, John smiled. He was certain Scarlet would like the blue-eyed puppy.

The next day John took the dog with him to the campground where he was completing work on another cabin. As John drove up to the little cabin in front that did double duty as Scarlet's abode and the office for the cabins, Scarlet came out and started to humorously chide John for being late. Then she saw the puppy in his hands and stopped short.

"What have you got?" she demanded.

"Your new best friend," replied John.

"You got a dog?" Scarlet said.

"No. I got *you* a dog," replied John with a big smile.

"I... I don't need a dog." stammered Scarlet.

"Scarlet dear, you need this dog," John said, as he stepped in close where Scarlet could see the puppy and his remarkable blue eyes.

"Oh, those eyes...he's looking right at me just like..." She murmured as she took the dog in her arms and hugged it. "Just look at him. It's a 'him' isn't it?" she said as she held the animal at arm's length to get a complete view of him. "I've never seen anything quite like him. What is he?" she asked.

"He's a Weimaraner," replied John. "What are you gonna call him?"

"He's Baby Blue Eyes, isn't he? You're my Baby Blue Eyes, puppy. Oh, I love him! I feel better somehow with my Baby Blue Eyes near me. Mmmm...." Scarlet hummed as she held the puppy.

John had never seen Scarlet so happy. Never!

"He surely is pretty," said John. "Not just his eyes, either. Look at how his coat shimmers somewhere between silvery and coppery. I knew you'd love him, Scarlet. I knew as soon as I saw him. I'm so glad you're happy. I... I... I love...." John stopped himself before he said any more. He just smiled at Scarlet, but there was a sadness behind the smile.

Scarlet didn't seem to notice what John had almost said. She continued to fuss over the puppy.

John suddenly feared he was destined to forever smile sadly when Scarlet was on his mind. Would he now and forever be the devoted, unrequited lover of Scarlet Hall? The puppy in Scarlet's arms turned to look back at John. Baby Blue Eyes knew! The puppy's look gave John the courage to say. "Scarlet, I love you and I want to be with you forever. Please marry me."

"Okay," she answered simply as if it was an everyday question. They both looked at each other with their surprise. In a moment they were rushing into each other's arms, shuffling the puppy between them. They never let go of each other. Scarlet threw an Afghan in a clothes basket, covered the sleepy puppy and returned to John's embrace. Delicately, they slithered out of their clothing and moved to Scarlet's bedroom where they fell into the warmest possible human embrace. Hours later, they fell asleep in each other's arms.

Later still, when John awoke, his first thought was, *Damn, I forgot the music. Oh, well. We can start over.*

John actually had a good voice and by the next day he had managed to remember the words to *Scarborough Fair*, which he sang over and over to his beautiful lady.

Three days later John and Scarlet emerged from her cabin. They walked hand in hand down to Peggy's Place, where they calmly entered and took an empty booth.

Clair walked up to the booth the pair had chosen and calmly said, "Hi, kids. What'll you have?"

"Scrambled eggs, bacon, toast and coffee," said Scarlet.

"What for you, John?"

"The same, except hot cakes instead of toast," John's voice was just a coarse whisper.

"Hot tea might be better for that voice," Clair commented.

"Okay," John said meekly as Clair walked off the give Peggy the order."

Moments later, Mr. Franklin walked in and took

the booth closest to the couple. Next, Scarlet's brother popped in, followed by Miss Annabel Lee, who was accompanied by her perennial fiancé, Brett Stephens.

By the time their food arrived, half the town of Winsome had crowded into Peggy's Place to witness the event of the season. The other half of the town were clamoring outside in the street demanding an appearance by the couple.

Mr. Franklin finally asked the couple when they planned to marry.

"We haven't actually talked about marriage, but I'd like it soon," said Scarlet looking up at her lover with wondering eyes.

"Who can marry us?" was John's instant reply.

"As mayor of Winsome, I have that authority," said Mr. Franklin. "How about next Saturday?" said the mayor.

John and Scarlet looked at each other, then at Franklin, and said simultaneously, "Okay."

From behind the counter, Peggy piped up, "Why don't we do it right here at the diner? We can do it out on the front steps. We can block off the street and there will plenty of room."

The day would become remembered as "The Winsome Block Party and Scarlet-John Wedding." As a Wedding Gift, the town collected enough money to build Annie's Place. It would be a haven, which Scarlet, Peter and John designed in the campground to give comfort and security to persons in deep peril.

Because of John's design, the cabin would seem to unfold to reveal rooms within rooms instilling feelings of safety to those entered. (It would require a trained guide to enter, for without a guide an uninvited person could only find exits.)

Scarlet Hall and her older brother, Peter, had wandered into Winsome as children on the run. Finding succor in Winsome, they never left and they now have time, finally, to cry for their stillborn sister, Annie, lying under a sycamore tree somewhere beyond Winsome.

SARA'S OPTION

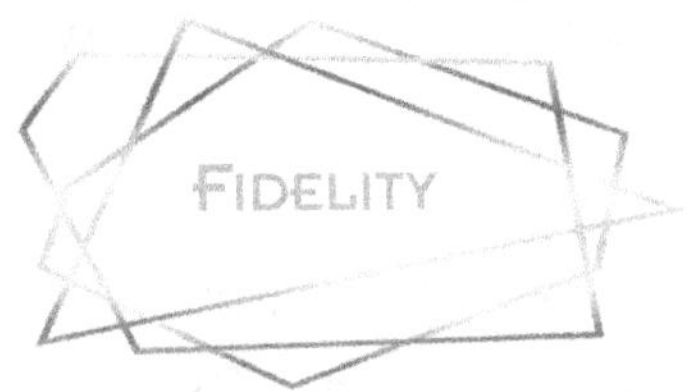

I feel like I'm running away from home," Sara laughed as she tucked her bus ticket into the pouch of her overnight travel bag. She looked at her husband who grinned back.

"Hey," Paul said, "You're a grown woman who can do as she pleases. Or have you forgotten all the rhetoric you've been quoting from your consciousness raising group? Besides, I don't think a bus ride for a weekend in Reno with an old college girlfriend can quite be listed as running away." He leaned near her and spoke very confidentially, "You know whatever you and Pam decide to do in that wicked city is all right with me." The teasing look remained in his eyes, "As long as you share all the details when you get back!" It was a continuing joke shared during their marriage.

"Paul, you're a voyeur at heart!" Sara grinned as she pursed her lips in a kiss and then looked out the window for the bus. The spring fog made Sacramento

Valley dismal, but she knew the drive up the mountains would be crisp and clear.

Sara was glad that this meeting with Pam would be so different from the meeting two years ago when Pam had flown to Sacramento for a job interview. Between planes, the school days friend took a taxi and arrived at Sara's front walk. Pam was striking in her three-piece executive suit, her carefree hairdo, and with a PH.D. behind her name.

While watching her former roommate come up the walk, Sara gained another twenty pounds, her hair frizzed, the dog developed fleas, and the edge of the carpet frayed. For those few moments Sara wondered why she had quit college, how she let herself gain that weight with the two children, and what could she possibly say of interest to this successful woman who used to be her best friend?

Communication was no problem as the two women hugged and continued the conversations only temporarily interrupted by ten years separation. After dinner, Paul tended the children in their bedtime routines, letting the friends talk. Sitting in the den, the two women could barely hear Paul's deep voice reading the bedtime stories.

"Your home is wonderful, so warm and inviting. Just like you dreamed of when you were dating Paul. And your children... just as sweet at their Dad!" Pam reminisced. "I remember you and Paul fell in love at first sight. I believed you were foolish to settle on just one man, even such a dear one. Now I envy your family and home," she finished with a sadness in her voice.

Sara thought she and Pam had merely chosen different priorities. "But Pam, you've accomplished your dream as well! You are a professor at a major University, being surrounded by intelligent co-workers, traveling the world for research."

"A dream is something you do in the night... in the dark... alone... usually alone." Pam paused, then shook her head and changed the subject.

By the time she took Pam to the airport that evening, Sara's split ends had grown back together, she lost twenty pounds, and the carpet fluffed up. The dog still had fleas, but Sara planned to remedy that as soon as possible.

This Friday afternoon, Sara sat at the bus station with a new Bachelor of Arts behind her name, in a trim suit that Paul had given her to celebrate her successful diet. At 34, Sara felt like she was beginning another facet of life. It felt so good inside herself to be competent with her family and embarking on new goals—whatever they might be.

Today was a beginning. Pam would be in Reno, Nevada for a consultation and had wondered if Sara could meet her there for girl talk. Sara had never been away from the family except for birthings at the hospital. It was just not something that had come up before. Paul had urged her to go.

"Sara, it's just for the weekend. Go ahead. You've had a rough time with the schoolbooks this year and deserve some time away. Besides, it will give you a chance to show off your new figure and you always have a good time with Pam."

"But Tim has soccer Saturday morning and Lynn was going to a party at..."

Paul interrupted her. "Hey Babe, we can handle it. We've learned to do a lot this year while you were in school. It was good for all of us. Take some time for yourself. You're a big girl now, it's time to leave the nest."

Sara's reluctancy turned to anticipation as she texted Pam she would meet her in Reno Friday night. When the bus rolled in, Paul helped her with her coat and walked her to the gate. He put his arms about her and held her back to look seriously into her face as he said, "You know, you're even more interesting a woman than you used to be. Maybe I shouldn't let such an attractive woman go off..." His kiss goodbye took on a remembered intensity and he held her a few moments longer. "You have a good time and say hello to Pam for us!"

The bus moved smoothly through the traffic until it reached the freeway and began the climb through the scenic foothills and gold country of California. Sara relaxed and enjoyed the sense of non-responsibility she felt. Over the last two years she had begun to realize that it would be possible for her to enjoy both family and a career. Tim and Lynn had taken on more responsibility and had enjoyed telling people they were putting their mother through college. The decision was solidified as Sara was being a class mother at Tim's school. Getting her station wagon ready to drive students to Sutter's Fort, Tim asked, "Mom, can't I go on a field trip by myself?" It was a son wanting to leave the nest. Sara sold the wagon and signed up for the classes she needed to fulfill a degree.

This simple trip to Reno was like an adventure. She remembered the first time she had ever driven the car alone. There was a sense of exultation at the awesome responsibility and the delicious feeling of being free on one's own. She realized that she was grinning even now as a voice spoke to her from across the aisle.

"You look as though you've got a good reason to be satisfied with yourself."

Sara turned to see a man dressed in stylish but soft denims, sweater, and shirt jacket smiling at her.

"Yes, I am!" Sara said enthusiastically. "I feel good." She hadn't noticed the man before, he must have gotten on at the Auburn stop in the foothills. He looked to be about her age and was traveling alone except for a paperback book in his hand.

"Oh," Sara said with interest, "I didn't know he had another book out."

"What?" The grey eyes looking at her were confused.

Sara turned sideways in her seat to better look at the traveler. Even now in mid-afternoon he showed a five o'clock shadow on his tanned face. His brown hair was just beginning to show some salt and pepper. *Like mine,* she thought as she said, "Your book." She nodded towards his paperback. "He's one of my favorite authors. I've been so busy with textbooks this year I haven't noticed the new novels out."

"You enjoy science fiction?" he asked.

"I like all fiction. The only kind I can't get into are detective mysteries. I think what I like best about science fiction is its variety and philosophies." Sara spoke easily to this man ready to go on into a dissertation on the philosophy of novels in today's world. *Oh oh, she thought, here I go sounding like Philosophy 314B. From housewife to expert lecturer, I guess that's what happens to 34 year old women in college.* She paused, smiled, and then retreated to looking out the window on her side. What was she doing chatting away like this? *But then again, why not!* She felt good, the weather and scenery were perfect and she was on holiday.

As Sara glanced back across the aisle the man was standing and asking, "Would you mind if I sat here?" He gestured to the empty aisle seat next to her. His smile was calm and waiting and instinctively Sara smiled back. For an answer she removed her coat from the seat and his tall frame slipped next to her.

"How far are you going?" he asked

"Just to Reno."

"Do you live there?"

"No, I'm meeting a friend."

"Lucky man?" he questioned quietly.

Sara laughed lightly but did not answer the implied question. This teasing talk was something she had not shared with a stranger since early college. It was fun to feel so young again. The jokes with Paul were comfortably established over years of marriage.

"Actually I'm meeting a Doctor, a Ph.D." She returned and then looking directly at him, "And you?"

"I teach in a high school in Auburn and when I think I can't stand the sound of one more teenager saying 'ya know…' I take the bus to Reno and enjoy a few shows, some gambling and regain my sense of humor."

"I've never thought of Reno as that humorous."

"Watching some of those adults with the slot machines can make a person think teenagers are the wisest people in the world!" He laughed easily then. He didn't seem to push the conversation, just talked to pass the driving time. Sara found it to be a different feeling talking to this stranger who looked at her so directly. It had been a long time since any man had looked at Tim's mother or Paul's wife that way. Maybe, she thought a bit surprised, he's looking at me.

"I'm David Locke," he smiled. He did not put out his hand and for that Sara was glad. Being a "new woman" Sara still wasn't sure whether to put out her hand, nod, or whatever when being introduced.

Sara returned the smile with, "I'm Sara Davenport." That was it. She couldn't think of anything else to say. She couldn't remember how the little talk games used to go but felt the need to say something.

"How's the poison oak this year?" she blurted. *Good grief, where did she get that?* "I mean, I always think of Auburn and Poison oak..."

"It's just fine,thank you," David said somberly but with a twinkle in his eyes.

Sitting that close to him, Sara could hardly move away. Instead she laughed, mostly at herself but even more at the situation. "I'm glad to hear that," she replied and then turned to look at the mountains moving by the window. They had been out of the fog for some time now and were winding through the winter of the Sierra Nevada range. David opened his book and the two rode in a comfortable silence for a while.

Finally David's voice broke through Sara's self reflection. "Are you married or... anything?" David asked her earnestly.

Sara turned to this man she had just met with a quizzical look on her face. She was confused. Everyone knew she was Paul's wife. Her left thumb bent across her palm to stroke her wedding ring. It was gone! She looked to her finger quickly and then remembered her ring was being resized at the jewelers and she must pick it up next week. In a flush, she realized this man did not know her as Paul's wife—to him she was just Sara. He was interested in finding out more. She couldn't remember such a compliment. She had been wife and mother for so long, she didn't know how to accept this interest in her as a woman. This was worth the anguish her diet had cost her. She looked again at her naked left hand and began to stammer an answer.

David took her confusion to be hesitancy or pain and he rushed on, "...I'm sorry, I didn't mean to pry. I just enjoy talking to people on these bus trips and you seem special... whoa, that sounds like a real come on... look, just forget it." David seemed uneasy now and he got up to swing himself over to his own aisle seat. "Have a nice trip," he smiled, and returned to his book.

Sara turned to the safety of her own window again, the setting sun marking shadows beneath the pines. She felt flustered inside. Occasionally during their marriage Sara would ask Paul if he took her for granted. Now she realized she had taken herself for granted. She was the one who thought of herself as "mother" or "wife." In their close social group, men never made passes at her. If anything, they would get her aside at a party to talk with her about other women, their wives or lovers. Sara was a good pal to talk with. Once Paul had said he thought Allen from the office was taken by her and Sara had accepted it as a joke. Where would she take anyone, she had laughingly thought. But then she remembered the way Paul had looked at her at the bus stop. *Oh,stop being silly,* she chided herself. *Paul loves you so of course he sees you as an attractive person. But then, maybe you are.* What a new thought. Sara had never had much time or interest in personal vanities. She had just accepted herself as average but lately men had treated her differently. The way Paul now looked at her was as if seeing someone new. A client of Paul's had complimented her on her directness and lovely hazel eyes. One of her professors had even commented on her quick mind. She had been so busy doing these past two years that she hadn't taken time to step back and re-evaluate. Who was Sara Davenport today? Her B.A. and name on the Dean's list demonstrated that she was intelligent. Her new suit showed her to be a determined woman (oh, that diet) who was confident in her good taste. But this encounter on the bus, her flustered feelings, these left her stumped.

In the twilight, Reno's lights were already shimmering as the bus came down from the mountains and rolled into the downtown station. Gathering her things, trying to put on her coat, Sara backed into the aisle and right into David.

"Here, let me help you," he said and touched her hand as he took her overnight bag, and carried it out of the bus.

Sara tried to think of a witty reply and said, "Thank you." *Oh, I've got a quick mind all right!*

"Can you meet your friend all right?" he asked as he handed her the travel bag and picked up his shaving kit.

"Yes, she said we'll meet in the lobby of that hotel—I can walk..."

He grinned and she realized she had dropped her air of mystery when he said, "I hope you and she will have a good time. Maybe I'll see you going home," and with that he was gone.

Sara watched David cross the street toward the hotels and casinos and wondered what it would be like to date again. That was definitely a man worth dating!

At the lobby desk Sara picked up her reservation and a message from Pam, "Sorry, business delay. I'll meet you at the hotel at 5:00 p.m, tomorrow, Saturday. Enjoy yourself! Pam."

Disappointed, Sara went up to her room and wondered what she could do for twenty-four hours. She had never been much of a gambler, and going to a casino show wouldn't be any fun alone. How did she used to entertain herself before her husband and ever-present family? She couldn't remember. She wondered what Paul was doing now. Reno was an exciting city, surely this new woman could find some-thing. She freshened her make up, hung up her extra blouse, and thought about calling Paul. *Don't be silly, she thought, you've only been gone a few hours. Anyway, Paul would be taking the kids out for Pizza tonight.* Sara texted him of her safe arrival, Pam's agenda, and she would be at dinner.

Sara went downstairs, past the slot machines and their perpetual clicking. The weekend crowds were already manning the bandits in force. Rather than take the buffet, Sara went on to the main dining room so she could be served. She began to enjoy the uniqueness of dining alone and settled in for some serious people watching. She was observing the lighted Keno board to decide how it was different from Bingo when a man stepped in front of her line of vision.

Looking up, she saw that David too had freshened up, shaved, and now was smiling down at her. "Did you meet your doctor all right?" he asked.

Sara hesitated. In this of all cities, how much of a gambler was she? She made her bid. "No, Pam's delayed til tomorrow." Then she waited.

David asked, "May I join you or do you have other plans?"

"Well, I've already ordered…"

"Don't worry, you can pay for it." He put his hands up as to surrender as he sat across from her. "I know better than to pick up checks, makes a woman think all sorts of things."

Sata wasn't sure why, but teasing with this man was so easy that she felt as though she wanted to play the game."What sort of things?"

"Well," he said expansively, "They try to jump my body. Hands all over me, sometimes, you'd be surprised. Those young women that a man meets nowadays are just animals. It's difficult for a man to just find a woman to talk to. About science fiction, for example."

Sara laughed openly at him. "You came all the way to Reno to talk science fiction?"

"And you came to meet a woman doctor?"

"All right, David Locke…"

"Ah, you remembered my name."

"Order your own dinner, and we'll talk about my favorite author and…"

"Young women wanting my body?"

"Not interested."

"Then who do you think will get the Hugo award for Sci-Fi this year?" He grinned as the waitress came for his order.

To Sara's surprise they did talk science fiction, about professors at the college in Sacramento, the property tax relief bills, and the prospect of drought. He was a high school teacher with funny anecdotes about students. As they finished eating, announcements blared for the entertainment soon to begin at a special pavilion outside.

"When was the last time you went to a circus?" David asked.

"Years and years unless you count the Kiddy Circus at the park," Sara answered.

"Then we'll go tonight!" he said, ushering Sara out of the restaurant to the elaborate tent next door. Crowds heightened the excitement of the event.

They took their seats and Sara was enthralled by the music, the expansive sets and the parade of performers. The acrobats strutted in the opening procession, tumbling on cues, dancing—always to the advantage of the spangled costumes. Sara felt the thrill of a child's first circus intermixed with an adult's admiration for the complexity of the awe inspiring performances. Magicians, clowns, and trapeze artists all vied for attention.

Watching an aerial performance, one flyer missed the hands of her catcher and started to fall. Sara gasped and grabbed David's hand. The flyer recovered because it was part of the thrills being performed. Sara looked down at her hand in David's then up to his smile. Quickly she dropped her hand and turned her attention back to the spectacle. She wasn't used to grabbing a hand other than her husband's!

Performances ending, they went into the casino where David briefly tried his hand at roulette, while Sara watched people like the croupier—a young woman with a crew cut and three pierced earrings in each ear. When David quickly tired of that, he guided Sara to another area. Moving to the Blackjack table they passed a man in overalls and work shirt wearing an absolutely elegant beaver top hat as he placed chips worth hundreds on the felt table. David sat at the table to play, while Sara was fascinated by the dealer's hands. The young woman's hands moved with deliberate grace as if performing a precise ritual. She would shuffle, deal, and then stand holding the deck to her breast like the little matchgirl's last match.

David played moderately, never seeming to gain or lose to Sara's inexperienced eye. But she enjoyed watching as he calculated his odds, made his next bet and laughed with her when he won. He seemed to really enjoy what he was doing. His face was animated and he kidded and talked with the dealer.

He had none of the glazed look that so many of the gamblers took on after hours in the smoky, glittering casinos. Sara encouraged him just by being there.

By early morning Sara needed some air and David agreed a walk would feel good. Passing the slots they saw a woman working four machines while dressed in a kelly green jogging suit with white stripes. Her hair was in curlers under a green flowered turban.

"What's she doing here at 2:30 a.m.?" Sara chuckled as David noted her glance. "Did her jogging from yesterday get interrupted or does she go jogging at 2:30 every morning?"

Laughing, they pushed through the door out to the crisp night air and walked the bustling sidewalks.

"Things people do here make no sense," David mused almost seriously. "Everyone knows the whole state exists for their own fantasy, it's all Oz and they're all running from Kansas."

"Or Auburn?" she questioned.

"Or Sacramento. While you're here you can put on whatever role you don't dare back home. Just like the man putting on his beaver hat."

"You noticed," she said softly, pleased that he too had been sensitive to all the people about them.

He stopped and looked directly at her. They were standing on the bridge over the river and the neon was shadowed here, the air very moist. He did not touch her. She wasn't sure why or if she wanted him to. His grey eyes were serious and after a little bit of forever he said, "I've also noticed how little you've said about yourself. You've only talked about what you think about things, not how you feel."

"Maybe I'm not sure. I'm just learning to wear different hats in Sacramento, I don't know what to wear in Reno." She sounded more confident than the words inside her mind.

Softly he answered, "Whatever you pick... it will be beautiful." And without touching, they looked at each other.

Sara felt a rush inside her. This man, this stranger saw only the woman she had fully become and he had found her beautiful. Looking in the mirror of his eyes, she knew it was true. For years she had thought about what she would do "when she grew up." Somewhere that was lost with the children, the family, with Paul as a comfortable way of life. Now she knew as never before, she was grown up. She was complete and could take the personal responsibility for anything she wanted to do, for all the feelings she wanted to keep or share.

They walked silently back to her hotel. At her door David, silently traced the curve of her cheek with the tips of his fingers and asked, "May I come in?"

"Not tonight. I bought my own dinner, remember?" she answered gently.

"You don't want to put your hands all over my body like the other female animals?" he questioned but it was a friendly tease, not pushy.

"Yes, I do..." Sara began but as his expression changed she went on, trying to recapture the lightness, "but I respect you too much to make demands after our first date."

David smiled gently and said, "We can have our second date tomorrow. I'm easy on my second date."

"We'll see..." Sara promised and she took his hand from her face and squeezed it as she went into her room. Checking her cell, there was a text. "Busy day! Tim's soccer team won. Love and miss you. Call me." Sara hesitated to call and wake Paul. She would text him tomorrow.

The next day, David appeared at brunch and coaxed Sara into going to the famous antique car collection for the afternoon. She didn't know much about the cars but David colored their histories with anecdotes about the imaginary people who may have driven them. She thought of how much Paul would love the collection. She'd have to bring him sometime when her mother could babysit. She was surprised that it took old cars to bring Paul to mind.

Returning to the hotel, a message in the lobby from Pam said, "Sorry, love. Client scratched, I have to go to New York instead. See you next trip."

David moved very close to Sara seeing the disappointment on her face. "Your friend canceled?" She nodded. All day they had casually taken hands or brushed close to each other. Looking down at her he said, "It's too late for a bus home tonight. I know a quiet dark place where we can let our senses soar."

"Oh David, I..." she hesitated. It wasn't just a thought of Paul's love for old cars. The words "senses soar" brought Paul's face to her mind. He was her protector, lover, hero—holding her hand when the babies were born, working their frugal budget so she could be home with the children, staying up for nights with a sick child, getting her back into college. The passion and joy of making love had never waivered. Paul was the core of her contentment.

"Of course," he murmured romantically and then said, "the Planetarium has a new show. I always spend part of my weekend there!" Immediately relieved at his suggestion of activity, Sara nodded. She and Paul used to visit the Planetarium on the college campus. Sara and David spent the evening soaring with the stars. New digital telescopes expanded the cosmos previously dreamed about. She anticipated sharing the presentation with Paul.

Returning to the hotel, the two walked. They enjoyed the company of a lovely night with Reno's lights shining the way. Escorting Sara to her door David asked, "Does this second date count? Will you ask me in?" He stood very close, his breath a caress on her face.

Sara hesitated, then smiled and pulled away. "David, I have so enjoyed our time together, but this 'second date' ends as the first. Yes, I am definitely married. You have reminded me of the magic of a man I have loved for years. Thank you for a wonderful weekend!" She briefly kissed his cheek and entered her room, alone.

Sunday afternoon Paul met Sara at the Sacramento depot. As she got off the bus, he hugged her so hard she could have been gone for years. She smiled up at him knowing how much she loved this big and gentle man who let her be her own woman, who encouraged, and chided, and trusted.

"You look terrific!" Paul laughed breathlessly. "Did you have a good time?"

Sara beamed. "A wonderful time!"

Paul stopped and looked at this marvelous person

he had watched growing these last few years. She was just so beautiful. He wondered if she knew. Then he teased, "To be that wonderful, did you have an affair?"

Sara looked contented with a wisp of a smile. "No," she said gently. "But I could have..."

She kissed her dearest husband tenderly.

TENDRILS OF WAR

There are hurricanes and tornadoes, Santa Anna winds, and horrendous winds as forces of nature. They show up as icons on television screen weather reports. A breeze does not have its own icon but happens to be a cool respite on a summer day, or a breath of warmth on a cold one. Just as a draft of air can weave its tendrils into a life, the Selective Service Draft influenced lives.

The Viet Nam War was not a fragment—the war fragmented our country. Its tendrils permeated the 1960's. Where WW II was heroic for defeating the Nazis, Korea was almost forgotten because of the US involvement with Viet Nam. In the Cold War, the assassinations, the draft, counter cultures, burning draft cards, etc., etc., etc., stirred the United States into total disarray. Decisions had to be made, postponed, or endured.

Two brothers, Benjamin and Richard, experienced

FACETS of PERCEPTION

Viet Nam in far different ways.

The Selective Service Conscription was effective when Benjamin started college in the late 1950's at The University of Arizona, a land grant school. He received a college deferment which would end with graduation, and required him to take two years of Reserved Officer Training Corps (ROTC). The deferment gave Ben time, but "the draft" was always present if his grades slipped or he canceled his load of credits.

By his graduation, Ben and his high school sweetheart, Sharon, wanted very much to be married. The sweetness of young love had matured to a life commitment and desire. They planned accordingly. A spring evening on the campus created a perfect setting for a proposal for a summer wedding to accommodate Ben's draft eligibility. They had never joined the draft demonstrations that scoured college campuses those years. With the examples of fathers in World Wars, Ben and his fiancé accepted the responsibility. So did their parents and families.

Ben tested and was accepted for Officer training in the Air Force. They married on May 30 (then it was set as Memorial Day) and would have a month together before he left for training. Sharon would stay home for the summer, working for Pima County Recreation and teaching dance to kids in summer recreation. When Ben became an officer, she would join him, and they would follow where the Air Force would send them.

It made sense to the young couple who wanted desperately to be together. Except, "Life is what happens while you are making other plans" became Truth to Ben and Sharon for the rest of their lives.

In the early morning summer, Ben left his teary bride for the bus ride to the Induction Center at the state capitol in Phoenix. By evening, he returned to meet his surprised bride with news he was rejected from the Air Force due to a back injury in his youth. He was still eligible for the draft but was without a job and married.

Finding employment was difficult because Ben was still draftable. Employers were hesitant to take on employees who could be drafted but were guaranteed their job upon their return, by law. After a training program with the Railway Express Agency was canceled, he finally signed up to take the Federal Service Entrance Exam. He hoped to stay in Tucson, not wanting to leave families and Sharon was trying to complete her senior year at the University of Arizona. She was on a grant for war orphans which continued for the months needed to graduate.

When offers finally came in for various Federal services, none were close to home. They had to make a choice, and it was Hill Air Force Base in Ogden, Utah. It was the closest offer: Ben had knowledge of the Air Force, and it was located in the west. They loaded a U-Haul truck with newly-wed furniture, and moved away from their families. The Utah hills greeted them with the dynamic colors of Fall even though it was only early September. Within three days of arrival in the Salt Lake Valley, Ben drove to work through the first snowfall of the season, while Sharon stayed in a rental without heat. Their Bassett hound was shivering in his Arizona summer coat. Living in Utah was going to be very different from their Arizona home.

As a young husband, Ben was still on the Selective Service lists but deferred because he was married. The couple watched as the Viet Nam war escalated and national responses changed. Each decision was tempered by the shadow of the Draft, even to starting a family. Just before his 26th birthday when he would become ineligible, the Draft Notice arrived. After two days of medical testing in Salt Lake, including a visit to a cardiologist, he was declared 4-F without explanation. He could only obtain that information from his original draft board location in person. They grabbed a few vacation days to visit family in Tucson and he checked in at the local draft board. The file there stated he was 4-F due to a heart defect he never knew he had.

For years after, doctors were unable to confirm that diagnosis which so impacted their lives. One doctor said it must have been a clerical error and somewhere there was a draftee with a heart problem. Ben was not going to Vietnam. After all the years of living with that specter hovering over their lives, decisions and dreams were muted.

Ben remained with the Logistics Command of the Air Force in Sacramento, California as a project manager and instructor until retirement. He was never sent to Viet Nam but was totally involved daily with war and aftermath. Logistics provided the supplies to keep the aircraft flying. If a plane couldn't fly, it was filtered through NORS (Non Operational Ready Supply). Messages and teletypes would convey the problem, so would a phone call. Fear of disclosure kept the call official but the young voices would ask, "How's the weather there?" or "What's the 49ers or Giants last ranking?" They just wanted a voice from home, just from home. There was great conflict between Ben's original commitment in ROTC and Viet Nam.

Looking back at their lives, Ben and Sharon questioned some decisions. Could they have chosen more wisely? Remembering the influence of the Sixties and the adaptations made, "Life had other plans..."

With the conflict of the war, there was considerable controversy of student deferment. Some argued that it was a gimmick to let rich kids in elite colleges get out of the draft. It was also a way for working class young men to live at home, work menial jobs, participate in land grant schools and ROTC and get a higher education. The Deferment had rules and the draft was in effect when students graduated or declined to follow them. When Benjamin and Sharon's only son graduated from the University in the eighties, there was no draft.

Benjamin's younger brother Richard was also draftable in the sixties. A lanky, easy going kid, Rick graduated from high school but was at odds what to do next. He didn't want to go to college, he wanted to work with his hands. A buddy had enlisted and received a bonus for getting others to enlist. So, teenager Richard enlisted and applied for mechanical training with the U.S. Army. He thought of his father's WW II experience driving a 6X6 truck through Europe with the 3rd Army. The Army training would put him in good stead for life working with mechanics and engines. Again, life was what happened... "Ben, it's me..." Richard's voice over the phone so late at night was alarming. He was in basic training at Fort Ord, California, while Ben was now living and working in Sacramento.

"What is it? Where are you?"

"I'm at some restaurant on I-80. The Nut Tree," he answered hesitatingly.

"What are you doing there?

"I've left the army, me and another guy are leaving. We can't take it anymore." There was panic in his last sentence.

"You're AWOL!?" Ben almost shouted, disbelieving. Ben and Sharon had visited Richard at Fort Ord when he was in basic training and knew it was hard on him. He had been ill having respiratory problems and repeatedly hospitalized with soldiers returning from Viet Nam with destroyed bodies and souls. Their agonies wiped out the bravado of war and replaced it with panic. His plan of mechanic training had been rescheduled, then denied. Now, he was running away but he called his older brother.

Not sure what they said next, Ben told him he would come get him. They'd talk this out, wait for him. He did. The other recruit left Richard there and hitchhiked away. Arriving at the restaurant, Ben hardly recognized the shattered sibling waiting for him. Ben ushered his younger brother into a secluded corner of the mostly empty restaurant. The booth was a temporary safe-place where the two brothers could talk in low voices. Mostly, Richard talked and Ben listened. Richard was hesitant but then his feelings flowed, sharing with his brother: his dread of future combat, his anxiety, the ramifications of this night. The cries of pain of the young soldiers in the hospital haunted him, and always would.

"Ben, there was one guy there who'd had a mortar shell blow his balls off! He made it home because a medic stopped the bleeding but he'd never have kids. There's another guy who was blown out of an injection seat and it took both of his arms off in the cockpit. And... and... there were those guys who just sat and stared at a spot on the wall. We don't know what they did or was done to them. They're just teens like me, and their whole lives are changed. This war is real! I'm being trained to enter it." Thoughts of mechanic's school and traveling to far-away locations were dwarfed by the realization he could become one of the terribly damaged young men in an Army Hospital.

"How long before you…?"

"Oh, my time is all changed now. Because of my test scores and rotations, I've been re-assigned to Air traffic control training. I'm supposed to be Graduated in two weeks. Mom and Dad are already planning to come."

"Two weeks and the rest of your life! Let's think this through."

The re-assuring voice of an older brother said the right words, considered the possibilities, and acknowledged Richard's fears. Their father's story was remembered. He had enlisted in the Army prior to Pearl Harbor. With Patton's army he had driven through the invasion of North Africa, Sicily, Italy, France and was moving into Germany when the war ended. He was never injured. How would Richard's decision affect him?

"He'd understand, he was there! Now… I am too!"

This was the beginning of Richard's adult life and he would have to make the choice of how it continued. Did he want the life being AWOL in a time of war? Could he face the possibilities of staying in the Army?

Into the dawn, they talked. Finally, Richard took a pause and his hands quivered slightly as he said, "I've decided to go back. It scares the shit out of me, but I'll go back to the Fort. I'm not sure of the consequences but it's my decision!"

Ben drove his brother back to Fort Ord in the early morning and stopped near the main entrance. They looked at each other, both took deep breaths, and then Richard left the car. He casually walked through the gate with a wave to the guards, a few words were exchanged, and he disappeared. Later, he wrote, "The guard just waved me through and my Sargeant said I missed bed check, but I told him I was in the John and he said okay."

When the graduation from Basic Training came, Richard was there marching in uniform and his parents were there with Ben and Sharon. The family was moved by those beautiful young soldiers on the parade ground with their crisp uniforms and perfect formation. Not knowing what lay ahead of them, Viet Nam was a different war than their father's World War Two, but it was war.

Because of his good test scores, Richard was re-assigned to Army Air Traffic control and transferred to Kesssler Air Force Base in Mississippi. Specific training followed at Fort Rucker, Alabama where he was chosen to be traffic controller for Army helicopter pilots who played such an intricate part in the Southeast Asia battles. He met a girl in Alabama, they married and started a family. He never went to Viet Nam. Later, a more mature Richard said he sometimes felt he missed something in the experience. Meeting veterans of the conflict, his view of the conflict altered. He never elaborated. He never became a civilian air traffic controller, or a mechanic. He died at age 30 in a highway accident, leaving behind a young son and daughter.

The above stories are not the plots for action screen movies or soul searching life changes. They are the fragments of a questionable war that made major alterations everyday to influence personal lives.

On January 27, 1973 the Draft was ended and the armed forces have been all-volunteer since then. The Selective Service still requires registration in case of national emergency.

Friends, acquaintances, schoolmates. All were affected by the fragments of Viet Nam. The tendrils of this war impacted our nation. Protestors set examples. Families were disrupted. Young men and women escaped to foreign countries. Government officials were called to task. Rights and responsibilities were debated. Social changes became trends. The tumultuous period of the Viet Nam War will be re-evaluated, historically dismissed, or even repeated. Its fragments changed the lives of generations. Painfully, it ended too many lives before they began.

The names of over 58,000 men and women are enshrined on the Vietnam Veterans Wall in Washington DC. (www.nps.gov/vive) No one knows how many lives were dramatically changed by a draft to a war few wanted, and few understood.

CHRISTMAS IN THE DESERT

ONCE UPON A TIME many, many years ago, Judy was a little girl living in Tucson, Arizona with her Mommy and Daddy. (Little brother wasn't born yet.) Judy was four years old.

That Christmas, Judy started to worry a little bit as little girls often do and Judy most of all. She worried a little bit because Tucson was not at all like the Christmas pictures on cards, on signs, or in the decorations in the stores. Tucson did not have any white snow... it had brown sand. There were no trees with mistletoe... there were cactuses. Big trucks brought layers of living Christmas trees to corner lots where they were sold for the holiday. The only snowmen around were made of tumble weeds stacked up and spray painted white. Her really big worry was about Santa coming down the chimney. Her house had no chimney so how would Santa get into her house now and all other Christmases in her life?

Judy tried to ask Santa that question when she saw him at the department store, but he just said, "Ho! Ho! Ho! I'll take care of it!"

When Judy asked her mother, Mommy said, "Oh, Santa knows all about chimneys. He just comes in the front door if the house doesn't have one."

"But without snow how can the reindeer pull Santa's sleigh?" Judy worriedly asked her daddy.

Daddy said with a smile, "Old Santa has many ways of travelling around. The reindeer are just his favorites. They can rest while he travels other ways, then they pick him up and travel on through Christmas Eve."

Judy finally talked to her good friends, Penelope and Oliver and told them how worried she was. Penelope was older and wiser. She was ten. She said she was sure the grown-ups knew what they were talking about. Oliver, who was seven, agreed with his sister. He was almost as tall as Penelope but still knew she was wiser about Christmas. They both smiled, but Judy could only frown.

Then something very big began to worry Judy and push all the little worries out of her mind. Mommy and Daddy said that Granma and Granpa wanted Judy and her cousin Marilyn (who was way older) to stay overnight at their house on Christmas Eve. All the grown-ups thought it would be fun for the cousins to have Christmas morning with Granma and Granpa. Now Judy was really worried because how would Santa find them? Mommy and Daddy and Granma and Granpa all said, "Santa will find you!"

So it was that Christmas Eve and Judy was still four years old. She was at Granma and Granpa's house which also did not have a chimney. Her way older cousin Marilyn, didn't seem to worry about chimneys so Judy worried for both of them.

Christmas Eve gets very dark, very early and it was at twilight when Granma asked Granpa to walk down to their little country store. She asked him to get some milk for breakfast in the morning and for Santa's snack that night. So Granpa walked to the store with Marilyn on one side and Judy on the other. They were halfway to the store when who should they see coming out of a house but Santa Claus! Marilyn laughed to see him and Granpa called out, "Hello Santa!" and Judy hid behind Granpa's leg. Little girls weren't supposed to be seen when Santa delivered toys. They were supposed to be home fast asleep!

Santa was dressed in his red velvet suit, with white fur down the front and around his cuffs. His beautiful red hat had a snowball of fur on its tip and a big black belt was buckled around his belly. His white beard fluttered as he moved about. He had a bag over his shoulder, and he stopped when he saw the evening walkers.

"Ho, Ho, Ho! Hello there!" Santa greeted them in a voice so happy, Judy had to peek around granpa to see him. "Merry Christmas to you all!" Santa called out.

Marilyn and Granpa returned the greeting but Judy for once in her short life was silent. Then, Santa opened the trunk of the car in the driveway and put his bag inside, he winked at Judy. "I'd love to visit with you but I have a busy night ahead. Merry Christmas!" He got into the driver's side and waved at them again as he pulled out onto the street. It was just like daddy said. Santa could travel other ways. Santa could go in and out of front doors if the need arose.

What about little girls being home in bed? she asked herself in a worried panic. *Santa will finish the houses on this street but I won't be at Granma's house. He won't find me there!*

Now, Judy knew what it was like to *really* have something to worry about. Granpa told her it was all right but she wanted to forget the milk and just go home. When they got to the store, Judy kept pulling Granpa's hand. They had to hurry and they cut across a desert lot so Santa wouldn't see Judy was still up and awake. When they got home they told Granma all about Santa and Granma was so tickled she smiled and smiled. The house smelled like fresh cookies and pine from the tree in the corner.

Judy wanted to go to bed right then but her grandparents told her she had to have some dinner first. Then they wanted to talk and tell stories and look at some pretty lights on their Christmas tree. Judy worried and worried.

Finally the grown-ups and Marlynn who was way older, helped Judy set out some milk and cookies. It was a relief when everyone let Judy scurry into bed and try to go to sleep faster than ever in her four years.

The next morning, very early. Judy woke up to find Mommy and Daddy and Granma and Granpa all waiting around the Christmas tree. There were lots of toys and presents for everyone to share. Santa did find them! He found them in Tucson at Granma and Granpa's house without a chimney, without snow, and without reindeer. He found them with the people who loved each other the most in the world.

And Judy never had to worry about Christmas again—even when she was way older.

THE LIGHT IN COLBY WOODS

Brett Stephens quietly opened the door to let Gertie out on the back porch. "Go on, Gertie, go out." The little dog just looked at Brett in refusal. The dog and the man went through this silly ritual every night before bed.

Brett stared at the little animal. He could not understand why the dog would not use the dog door he had laboriously installed for her to get in and out by herself. Brett really loved the little dachshund, but he still had a lot to learn about dogs.

Why was she so stubborn every night? Why was she always stubborn and independent. Didn't she realize how small she was? How fragile? No, of course not. She thought she was indestructible. Small dog, giant ego.

Brett gave up, picked the dog up and carried her across the porch, down the steps and deposited her on the grass. Gertie had won the battle of wits once more. Brett never seemed to grasp the idea Gertie loved the attention her recalcitrance garnered. All he knew was if he carried her out to the grass she would wander around in the cold for several minutes sniffing for the perfect spot to pee, after which she would run back to the door and bark demanding entry.

Tonight, the rest of the ritual didn't happen. Gertie ran back to the rear fence and began to growl. The change in the dog's behavior surprised Brett and he looked beyond the fence where the dog's attention was focused.

There was a light in the woods.

There should not be a light out there. Those woods were very dense all the way up to the distant cliffs. Nobody lived there. There was no good reason for anyone to be out in Colby Woods on this cold night. As his mind raced through possibilities, apprehension began to seep over Brett. This just seemed wrong. Everything about Colby Woods always seemed wrong. Those woods were just creepy. Of course, many things around the little town of Winsome seemed tilted out of focus and just a bit strange.

"Why am I even staying here?" Brett asked aloud to himself. "I don't know if I really like this place." Brett had stopped in the little town of Winsome on a whim because Gertie whined pathetically as he drove through the village. She seemed insistent that he stop.

After college Brett's parents suggested a trip, a sort of personal voyage to start the next phase of his life. His parents had given him a car for graduation. It was a plain green Chevy sedan. It was not new, but it was dependable. Mom and Dad had also given him enough money to last about a year if he was careful with it. Brett had worked hard for his degree in creative writing, now it was time to put it to work.

Brett had driven over two thousand miles on his odyssey of discovery, covering a good portion of the upper mid-west. His only companion on his journey was Gertie, the dachshund he had received for his fourteenth birthday. Gertie was eight years old now and was still vibrant and healthy. His parents thought Gertie's presence on the trip would help keep Brett focused on his quest.

Once in Winsome, he decided to stay for a while. Somehow, Brett felt drawn to this place which had an odd feeling of familiarity. The area seemed old and mysterious to him, perfect for a novel. He rented the little house on the outskirts of town near some woods. He thought this would be the place which would inspire him, but mostly because the rent was cheap.

Settling in with his meager belongings, Brett felt as if he had lived here before. The idea of reincarnation and prior lives always seemed silly to Brett. His Catholic upbringing did not condone such ridiculous nonsense. Still, he could not shake the strange sense he had been here before. There was just something about this place which disturbed him, and Gertie seemed to love the place.

Suddenly Gertie began to bark, snapping Brett back to the night's reality. It was not the usual irritating yapping she used to garner attention. This was visceral, loud and with purpose. A dachshund can make a lot of noise when it wants to. Brett became alarmed. What did she see? Or was it something she smelled? What was out there that disturbed Gertie so much?

Brett realized he was ill-equipped for a trudge through unfamiliar ground on a cold dark night. He decided to go back to the house and get better shoes and warmer clothes. He ran back to the house and into his bedroom still shivering and his teeth were chattering. He dug out his hiking boots and heavy socks, then pulled his heaviest coat from the closet.

What's wrong with me? Why did I get so cold so quickly? Maybe I'm getting sick, the thoughts raced through his head. Then he remembered Gertie. "Oh, I'd better go find her right away," he said aloud to himself. Brett added his driving gloves and a stocking cap from his closet. He grabbed the little flashlight he kept on the windowsill beside the door. He turned the heavy knob to step outside, pulling the door closed behind him.

Even with his warmer coat and stocking cap, the cold air embraced him. "Now where's that dog?" he muttered aloud as he trudged across the porch and down the steps.

Once on the ground he paused to listen for the dog's bark. Nothing. He set off toward the back fence calling the dog's name and whistling for her. *Not that she ever responds to me*, he mused.

The fence was more a formality than a real barrier. *Gertie had probably pushed her way under it*, Brett thought as he lifted one leg over the rickety fence, then the other. Now outside the yard, Brett could see almost nothing. *I should have brought a better light*, he thought as he cupped his hands around his mouth and resumed calling the dog.

"Gertie. Here, girl. Come on, Gertie. Come on, don't play games tonight!" He heard nothing from the dog.

There was no light to see anything. It was the dark of the moon; the stars, while bright, didn't provide illumination down here in the woods. Brett stumbled on following Gertie, virtually blind in this darkness. He continued calling the dog's name and giving occasional sharp whistles in hopes of getting some response from his recalcitrant canine.

After falling for the third time and breaking his flashlight, Brett decided to go home and get a better flashlight, better gloves, and warmer clothing.

"Wait a minute," he said after turning around several times, "Where am I? Which way's home?" The woods were so dark Brett could barely see his own hands.

He could no longer see the glow he had been following, nor was he sure in which direction to head back to his house. He remembered something from boyhood. A technique about how to find one's bearings in the dark by turning slowly, step by step in a circle, which Scoutmaster Zemlicka had taught him as a kid. Brett decided to avail himself of that technique now.

Brett stood up straight, took a deep breath, then turned slowly to his left but seeing nothing, he stopped. After a brief pause, he continued to turn more to his left, still nothing. So much for that idea, it didn't work in the woods.

At that moment Gertie barked, just one short, sharp, "Woof." Brett wasn't sure which direction the sound came from. Then came another, "Woof." That focused Brett and he moved toward the sound until Gertie met him with a soft grumbling bark. He bent down to pet her, but she hurried off, glancing back at him as if she wanted him to follow her. Looking up in the direction Gerti was heading, Brett saw the glow again.

It was a strange light, more of a glimmer than a clear light. It was good enough for Brett. He kept his focus on the glow as he stumbled on and he fell again. Struggling on, following the glow and Gertie's woofs, Brett finally reached a small clearing.

The light he had been following came from a window of a cabin. Brett had never suspected there was a cabin in these woods. Who could possibly live here? Why had he never been told there was someone living in these woods? What if it was someone dangerous? The blood was pounding in Brett's ears.

Wait a minute, he thought to himself, *it doesn't have to be someone dangerous. I've seen too many horror movies. I'll knock on the door.* Brett walked up to the door and knocked loudly. There was no response at first, but after a moment, a soft feminine voice responded, "Yes, who are you? Who's out there?"

A woman! Out here, alone in these woods! Brett was stunned. *What should I say to her? I'll just say who I am. That's all.*

"My name is Brett Stephens. I live beyond the woods. I was looking for a small dog which ran off, then I got lost. I didn't know anybody lived out here. All I need is directions how to get out of these woods," Brett said, hoping he didn't sound like a crazy axe murderer loose in the forest and making up a dumb story about a lost dog.

After a few moments the door of the cabin opened a bit and the woman said, "I will come out just long enough to tell you how to get out of the woods. Will you promise me you are a gentleman?"

"Yes, of course, I promise," said Brett, thinking to himself, *My god, how naïve is this woman? She's lucky I'm a decent man.*

The door swung open, and a beautiful young woman cautiously stepped over the threshold. Brett could see the cabin behind her was lit by candles, many candles.

The young woman said, "My name is Daisy. My husband is Robert Colby. He's in Fort Williams with his brother, looking to buy himself a car. I expect him home soon. He's been gone an awful long time."

The woman's speech was unusual, sounding kind of old fashioned. Her clothes were odd, as well. She had a high-necked blouse and full skirt which hung almost to the floor. Her hair was carefully pinned up on top of her head. She was holding a small lantern lit by a candle. It looked as if it had been made from a tin can.

Brett said, "I'm sorry I disturbed you; I just need directions on how to get out of these woods."

"It's alright, Mr. Stephens. I'm delighted to assist you."

What was it about her voice? It wasn't really an accent, but whatever it was, Brett found it charming.

She continued. "All you need do is follow the footpath over there," she said pointing off to her right. "It's about seventy paces, or so, down to the road. There's a big rock there. Turn left at the rock and the road goes all the way to the county seat in Fort Williams, should you desire to go so far. Please accept this lantern so you can see the footpath. Just leave it on the big rock down by the road. I'll collect it in the morning."

"Thank you, ma'am," said Brett. "Thank you so much for being nice to a stranger. Most people don't bother anymore."

"Oh, I wouldn't know about that, Mr. Stephens. I'm pleased to help," said Mrs. Colby.

Brett took the lantern, awkwardly waved goodbye to Mrs. Colby, and started off down the path through the woods. He soon came to the rock the woman told him about. The road was little more than two sunken ruts through overgrown weeds and brush, but it was just visible in the dark and was passable. Brett blew out the candle, then carefully set the little lantern on the rock and began what turned out to be a long walk home.

Brett finally arrived home exhausted. It was after two in the morning, and he was worried about Gertie, whom he hadn't seen since before he spoke to Mrs. Colby. Where had the time gone? Brett walked into his bedroom and found Gertie sleeping in the master's bed. Obviously, it had suited Gertie to use the dog door for once. As he approached the bed Gertie grunted gently, indicating she did not wish to be disturbed. Brett ignored the warning and reached to pull back the covers. Gertie grumbled again.

"Oh, shut up! A fine lot of help you were tonight," the man said as he pushed the dog to the other side of the bed, crawled in and pulled the covers over them both and went to sleep.

The next morning after a good hot shower, Brett fed

Gertie then shaved, dressed, and grabbed his car keys. He set off for Peggy's Place, in what passed for the center of Winsome, where he ordered a big plate of pancakes and sausages. While Clair, Peggy's sister and waitress, was taking his order, Brett mentioned he had been to a cabin in the Colby Woods last night.

Clair lifted an eyelid and stared askance at him and said, "What have you been smoking in that little house of yours, kid? There's no cabin in Colby Woods." Whereupon Clair marched off to the kitchen with Brett's order.

Brett spent several minutes watching a very tall, old man sweep the café floor. Finally, Clair returned and slid the big breakfast platter in front of him.

"Thank you," Brett said, then added, "I really did go to the cabin. My dog had run away, and I got lost in those woods trying to find her. I saw the light from the cabin and walked until I came to the clearing where the cabin is. I talked to a young woman who said she was Daisy Colby. She showed me how to find a road to get back home. Honest."

Clair took a step back, turned toward the kitchen and shouted, "Hey! Peggy! Come here. This kid's telling me a whopper."

Brett noticed the old man sweeping the floor had stopped his work and was eavesdropping on his conversation with Clair.

Peggy came out from the kitchen and walked to

Brett's booth. "Okay, this better be a good one, or I'll charge you double for wasting my time," Peggy grumbled.

Brett repeated the whole story of what had transpired the previous night. Peggy and Clair stared at each other a while, then Clair said, "It was the dark of the moon. That's always a strange time when strange things happen around here."

Peggy looked directly into Brett's eyes and an odd smile came over her face as she said, "Okay, kid. That was a good one. Breakfast is on me." Peggy turned and went back to her kitchen.

The old man commented, "Yep, that was a good one."

"What... What was that all about the dark of the moon? Why the free breakfast?" Brett asked Clair.

"There's a legend about those woods and the cabin, which, by the way, burned down back in the 1920s and killed Daisy Colby. Whatever happened to you last night, you just made our day with your tall tale," Clair answered, laughing as she walked back to talk with her sister.

"How can I find out more about this?" Brett begged.

Clair looked back over her shoulder, "Go talk to the librarian. She knows the whole story. Library's just down the road."

After finishing his breakfast, Brett started toward

the door. The old man sweeping the floor gave him a big smile and said, "Welcome to Winsome, young man. Enjoy your journey."

Brett smiled and said, "Thank you, but I'm not going on a journey."

The old man's smile got even bigger, and he said, "You'll see."

Brett wondered what the old guy meant by that, but he said nothing. He wanted to know more about the Woods and the Colby family. This just might be the basis for his novel.

The Winsome Library occupied an old army barracks left over from when troops were stationed in Winsome during World War II. It was a cold and drafty old building, kind of quaint in a small-town way. The sole employee of the library sat at a beautiful wooden desk with intricate hand carvings. An equally beautiful nameplate on the desk said, *Miss Annabel Lee — Librarian*. Brett wondered if the pretty young woman behind the nameplate actually bore the name or was it some sort of joke to identify her with Poe's famous heroine.

Brett approached the desk and said, "Good morning, Ms. Lee. I'm sorry to bother you. My name is Brett Stephens, and I'm looking for information about Colby Woods and the Colby Family."

Her eyes twinkled and a big smile filled her face as she said, "You're no bother, Mr. Stephens. Please call me

Annabel. You've come to the right place. I've been expecting you. Let's go look at the material we have on hand to answer your questions." She rose from her chair and led Brett off into the stacks.

Brett was puzzled as to how she could have been expecting him. Perhaps Peggy or Clair had given her a heads-up call. But why?

"These are copies of the Stone County Recorder's books," Annabel said, gesturing toward bookcases full of binders. "They're filed by date beginning with the 1880s, there on the left, and ending here on the right with the latest year. As I recall, Colby Woods was named in the 1920s following the big fire down there."

"The big fire?" questioned Brett, "I thought it was just the cabin. I need to know more about it. Peggy and Clair said you would be able to tell me about it."

"Yes, that sounds like something they would say. Anyway, a good part of the woods burned when the Colby cabin burned down. It was in 1926. We should probably start there," said Annabel.

Brett was wondering to himself if the cabin had been rebuilt, or if it was a different one from the one where Daisy had helped him last night. The thought of Daisy gave him pause. *What's going on here? Are these people playing a joke on the city boy?*

"Now, as for the Colby Family," continued Annabel. "The best place to look would be in the old Stone County Sentinel files," Annabel explained as she led Brett into the next aisle of books. "The Sentinel section is right here," the librarian said, pointing at bookcases loaded with more large binders of past issues of the Sentinel.

"The Sentinel was the old newspaper hereabouts. It was published from the early 1800s until it went bankrupt during the Great Depression." Annabel gave Brett another smile and added, "You can use one of the tables in the back. Just leave the binders on the table when you're finished. I'll put everything away. Have fun!"

Brett watched Annabel walk away. *Hmm, Annabel is a special kind of person. Sweet, smart... and sexy.* Brett snapped out of his lustful reverie. *Or is she playing a game with me?* Annabel had not even asked him why he was so interested in the Colby story, which seemed unusual. *Why do I feel I'm being played somehow?* He shrugged off the thoughts and decided to get to work.

Brett began with the Stone County Recorder's books where he discovered a map and a handwritten note dated April 11, 1927, which stated the unnamed woods between Winsome and the cliffs to the north would henceforth be named for its only residents, the Colby Family, who had lost their home and all their belongings in the Great Fire. There was no mention of deaths or survivors.

Next, he started searching the Sentinel binders where he found several news articles of interest. The first was regarding an attempted bank robbery on October 6,

1926, in Fort Williams. There were two robbers involved, who were identified as Robert Colby and John Colby, his younger brother, both of whom were residents of Stone County. Both men were shot and killed by the bank guard in the botched robbery attempt. Daisy had said her husband's name was Robert Colby. Brett was startled by the thrill of excitement racing through his body at the possibility of Daisy being widowed. He felt a twinge of guilt mixed with confusion because of his thoughts. *What's going on? How did I get in this... this nightmare?*

Brett also found several articles about the Great Fire in October 1926. As he read the Sentinel's reports of the fire, it became clear the fire had started in, or near, the Colby cabin, probably on October 21, 1926. The fire spread into the surrounding woods and stubbornly continued to burn for a week despite efforts to put it out, a powerful storm the following week finally extinguished the last of it. One article mentioned the only death associated with the fire was the young Widow Colby, who was never seen following the fire and was assumed to have been killed in the blaze. There was speculation Widow Colby may have started the fire accidentally while grieving the loss of her husband.

Brett sat staring at the rough interior wall of the old wooden library building. His thoughts centered on Daisy Colby, whom he had now fantasized into his perfect woman: She was near his age, pretty, sweet, helpful, and vulnerable. In Brett's daydreams he saw himself as Daisy's rescuer. He seemed to be developing a habit of daydreaming while shoving away reality. There was just something about this place.

Brett was startled back to reality by Miss Annabel Lee asking, "Did you find what you were searching for, Mr. Stephens?"

"Huh? Oh, yes. I got every... everything," he stammered, feeling guilty as if Annabel Lee might somehow be privy to his silly thoughts about the widowed Daisy Colby.

"I only ask, Mr. Stephens, because I want to make sure the Winsome Library is providing good service. It's the only reason I am here."

"Oh, Ms. Lee... Annabel, you've given me wonderful service..." *Oh, shit. That sounds like I'm thanking her for sex,* Brett thought as Annabel stood there and smiled down at him. *What do I do now?* Brett's mind clouded over leaving him incapable of neither speech nor rational thought. The young man just sat there holding his breath.

Sensing his discomfort, Annabel asked, "Mr. Stephens, are you okay? Take a deep breath. You're probably having a reaction to the dust on all these old books. Let me get you a glass of water."

"No, no, no, I'm... I'm... I'm okay," Brett stammered, completely flummoxed by Miss Annabel Lee.

"Mr. Stephens, do you mind if I inquire about the reason for your interest in local history? Part of my job here is being the local historian."

Brett paused, hesitant to tell last night's story again given the reaction of Peggy and Clair at the cafe. Still, somehow, he was compelled to tell his story to this woman.

Brett took a deep breath, then began, "I had a strange experience last night," he said. "It began with my dog, Gertie, running off in Colby Woods behind my house. I went after her because it was so cold, and I worry about her." He told the whole story and her reaction was similar to those of Peggy and Clair, but somehow different.

She probably thinks I'm some nut case, thought Brett as he hurriedly began gathering all his notes and papers and started toward the library door. The lovely Miss Annabel Lee followed a couple of paces behind him. As he reached the exit, Annabel stepped ahead of him and put her hand on the door preventing Brett from opening it.

Annabel said, "Dogs sometimes lead us where we never expected to go. I'll be more than happy to help you with anything you need, Brett."

Surprised by Annabel's comment about dogs and the use of his first name, Brett turned toward the young woman and said, "Thank you, Annabel, I look forward to our next meeting."

Annabel beamed with joy. Brett thought to himself, *Why did I phrase it that way? It came out sounding like a tryst.*

"Don't rush off, Brett," said Annabel. "I think we should discuss this some more right now. You are not the only person disturbed by Colby Woods. Please tell me what's bothering you so much."

Brett stood there in front of Annabel, his shoulders stooped, his voice shaky and unsteady. Slowly he began, "I was excited by her. I... I'm not sure why. I don't understand it. When I read in the old newspapers what had happened to her, I wondered if Daisy Colby had survived. I hoped she had. She was so young, so pretty, so vulnerable..."

Brett stopped speaking and just stood silent for several seconds, then said, "My God, what was I thinking? It's impossible for her to have been the same woman. Even if she survived the fire, she would be over a hundred years old! What is this? What's the matter with me? It must have been a different Daisy Colby down there in the woods last night. There's just no way it could be the one from 1926. It had to be another Daisy, perhaps her granddaughter. I have to go back to the cabin." It all came tumbling out of him for Miss Annabel Lee. Brett could not understand, but he was compelled in some odd way to tell her his story and questions.

Annabel reached out to Brett, she put her hands on both his shoulders. She looked directly into his eyes and whispered, "You are not alone, Brett. I would like to go to the cabin with you."

Brett was stunned. *Why would she do such a thing? This is crazy,* he thought to himself.

"Brett," said Annabel. "I told you; you are not alone. You are not the first person to be confused by Colby Woods and the cabin and Daisy Colby's story. I had a similar experience last year, which is why I haven't been able to leave Winsome." Annabel paused, then added, "Let's go to the cabin and see if we can settle this. You might want to bring your dog. I'd like to meet her. Besides, there's no telling where she might lead us." Annabel put on her coat and locked the library door as they left together.

While they were walking back to Peggy's Place where he had left his car, Brett thought, *It's probably lonely for her in a drafty old library alone all day. I wonder if there's a man in her life. Stop it, you dumbass! Don't you have enough to worry about without adding more to the mix?*

Annabel took Brett's hand and held it all the way to his car. Her gesture was comforting, yet eerie at the same time. *Who is this woman? What have I gotten into?* Brett's mind was racing.

Brett unlocked the Chevy, held the door for Annabel, then got in the driver's side, backed out of the parking space, and pulled out onto the road headed toward his house. At the driveway he shut off the engine, then said, "I'll just be a moment getting Gertie."

"Oh, no. I'd love to see your home, and I would

like to meet Gertie on her home turf. Dogs seem to like things like that," said Annabel.

What a strange thing to say, she seems to know something about dogs.

Once inside the house, Gertie was nowhere to be seen.

Brett said, "Gertie is probably in bed." As expected, Gertie was curled under the covers in the middle of his double bed.

"Get up, Gertie, someone wants to meet you," said Brett. Gertie yawned, stretched and jumped to the floor. As Annabel entered the room Maggie went into a play bow to impress the stranger.

"Oh, my! What a beauty!" said Miss Annabel Lee, smiling, and seeming genuinely impressed by the little dachshund. A few minutes later the three of them set off for Colby Woods in Brett's Chevy.

Driving from Winsome to Colby Woods he had to come to a stop. There was a gate across the road with a 'ROAD CLOSED' sign hanging on it. *That's odd. I don't remember a gate on this road last night,* Brett thought.

There was space on both sides of the road for parking. Brett pulled into a spot and shut off his engine. He, Annabel, and Gertie got out and walked up to the gate. Brett ran his hand along part of the road block. *I must have walked around it. I certainly don't remember it,* he thought.

When Annabel saw Brett touching the gate she

asked, "Is everything okay?"

"Oh, yes, I just have no recollection of passing by this barrier last night," said Brett, glancing at Annabel as he spoke. He was startled by the expression on Annabel's face. It looked like joy, terror, bliss and fear all rolled together.

"Annabel, are you all right?" asked Brett, alarmed.

"I'm sorry. I'm okay. I was surprised when you said you didn't remember the gate. Forget it. I overreacted," Annabel said. "Let's go on up the road."

Brett was still concerned about Annabel's reaction as he turned. Gertie bounded up the road ahead of the couple. Beyond the gate there were some informational signs where the woods began. One sign attracted Brett's attention. It said: "Path to cabin starts beside the big rock."

Wow, he thought, *Just the information we need.*

Brett automatically took Annabel's hand, and they started up the weedy road and soon saw the big rock.

"There's the big rock where the path starts," he said. "I wonder what happened to the lantern? I put it there last night just like Daisy Colby told me."

Annabel shook her head. Brett wondered why, but he said nothing.

When they got to the clearing, Brett stopped dead in his tracks. The cabin was nothing, just a burnt-out hulk. The old logs were rotted, and the signs of a fire were faint from the passage of time.

"How can this be?!" Brett asked aloud. "No, it wasn't like this last night," he added and his voice became forceful. "This is wrong. Just plain wrong! Daisy has to be here..." Brett said. He was completely baffled by the cabin's condition. "I know she was here. I saw her. I spoke with her. Where did she go?"

"I know, Brett. I understand," said Annabel.

Brett saw a plaque fastened to a post in front of the ruins. He walked over to read it aloud: "This is the Colby cabin. The Great Fire of 1926 began on this spot on the night of October 21, 1926, when Daisy Colby set fire to the cabin out of grief for her husband Robert. Robert had been killed, along with his younger brother John, a few days earlier in a failed bank robbery in Fort Williams. The body of Mrs. Colby was never found, it is thought her body was consumed in the Great Fire."

Brett stood reading the words on the plaque over and over. *This must be wrong,* he kept telling himself. *Daisy could not have done this.* Finally, Brett took a deep breath, turned and said to Annabel, "That is not what happened."

"Yes, it is, Brett," she replied.

"What? What do you mean? How could you know?" he snapped back at her.

"I know because... I seem to remember doing it," Annabel said softly. "I don't know how. I just remember a man knocking on the cabin door. I remember asking who it was. You promised you were a gentleman, and you were looking for a missing dog. I told you how to find the road. I gave you a little lantern because it was dark. A few days after you left, I was told my husband had been killed. Later, I threw a kerosene lantern in the cabin and started the fire."

"What? What are you saying?" Brett said in disbelief.

"I don't know how, but somehow, it's what I remember," she said. She was shivering now.

"Who are you? Why are you making up all these stories? What's your real name?" shouted Brett.

"Annabel Lee is my real name." Annabel began to cry. "Lee is my family name. My dad named me Annabel because he always liked Edgar Allan Poe's romantic poem," whispered Annabel, with tears beginning to stream down her cheeks. "Please don't be angry with me. I really don't understand what's happening here either," she said.

"Are you and those women at the cafe in this together? Are you all just making a fool of the city boy?" he shouted.

"No, Brett, please believe me. I don't understand either. I really believe I've met you before at the cabin," Annabel sobbed. She crumpled to her knees now, bent over pulling herself into a fetal position on the ground. "Don't hit me. Please Robert! Don't hit me, Robert!"

"Oh, God, please don't cry. I can't stand that," Brett whispered quietly as he pulled Annabel to her feet.

I'm sorry I yelled at you. I'm not Robert and I'd never hit you, Annabel. Never. We'll figure this out. Somehow we'll do it," He held her gently for moments then repeated, "Somehow, we'll understand." Gently taking her hand, Brett led Annabel back to his car.

It was warm in the car and Brett was pouring sweat. He and Annabel stayed there holding hands for a long time.

Finally, Annabel broke the silence. "Whatever is happening, it's getting worse. Since I came to Winsome, I've seen some strange things, but nothing like this. This place is just plain weird. I don't understand what we're supposed to do. What does all this mean?"

"I don't know," Brett said as he started the car. "Let's get away from here and go back to town."

"I don't want to go back to the library right now," said Annabel. "Can we go to Peggy's Place?"

"Okay," Brett replied. "Those two seem to know more about us than we ourselves do."

Brett put the car in reverse and started to back up. Suddenly, Gertie began to bark furiously and Brett realized he had left her out of the car. He opened the door and as she jumped in, he said, "What's your problem? You seemed to know the way home last night."

The little dog nestled between them on the front seat.

Ten minutes later Brett pulled into a parking spot at Peggy's. The lunch crowd had left and there were only two customers in the cafe. As the couple walked to an empty booth near the back, Clair followed them and asked, "Can I get you both something to drink? A couple of coffees maybe?"

"Yeah, two coffees. Please," said Brett.

"And some answers," added Annabel.

The other two customers paid their bill and left, Peggy locked the door and put up the "Closed" sign. Then she and Clair, each of them bearing two cups of coffee, came and sat opposite the young couple.

"What is happening to us?" Brett said to the sisters. His voice was plaintive and desperate.

"You've been out to the cabin, haven't you?" Peggy's voice had a tone of reprimand in it.

Clair added, "You'd best stay away from that place. It drives people nuts."

Brett stared at the two women, while Annabel sipped the very hot coffee. Brett began to speak, "Aren't you two going to say something? Anything? It has always seemed like you know so much about what goes on around here. Like you know something about us," Brett said, then paused, and lowered his voice. "Well? Let's have it! Something creepy or frightening? Go ahead, scare us!"

Annabel put her coffee cup down, a tear beginning in her eye.

Peggy spoke up, "Look, all we know are rumors, ghost stories, tall tales about the Colby Family.

Everybody here in Winsome knows these stories."

"What's going on in this town? I don't mean just about the Colby family. Why is everything creepy here? Why are you afraid to talk about it?" Brett calmed himself, looked at Clair and said, "Look, you told me to talk to the librarian. I went to the library and met Annabel. We talked about the town. We went to the cabin and it's nothing but a burnt-out ruin. It wasn't like that last night! What happened? Do you know anything about that?" He hoped his seriousness would encourage them.

Both sisters hung their heads and answered simultaneously, "No."

"Can anyone in this damned town explain it?" Brett pressed, he needed answers for his night's experience. "What is it about Winsome? I mean, who, or what runs this town? Huh? Please don't just sit there!"

Peggy's jaw was clamped shut and her face had become pale. Neither woman spoke. Annabel was almost sobbing. Brett considered throwing his now cold coffee at the two sisters but the prospective author controlled his frustration. "I need to know," he repeated.

"Don't blame Peggy or Clair. Neither of them is to blame for your situation, young man," a deep masculine voice boomed from behind the counter.

Startled by the seemingly disembodied voice, Brett jumped to his feet and called, "Who's there? Who are you?"

"Calm down, young man. My name is Lewis Franklin. I own this building. I am the oldest person living in Winsome, and sort of the honorary mayor." Brett turned and saw the tall, ancient figure standing behind the counter. It was the old guy who swept the floors.

Mr. Franklin spoke slowly, deliberately. "From before the time Winsome was founded, strange things have happened hereabout. Some say it's the water, or the enchanted woods. Nobody really knows. Sometimes you may see things that are not real, not actually where they appear to be. Native Americans are familiar with the place. Several nations send young members here for spiritual journeys."

"Winsome is just one of those spooky places which pop up in the world from time to time. The town has strange powers which cause anomalies, and right now you and Miss Lee are caught up in a big one."

"You are wondering if you are reincarnated or are some sort of time travelers. Isn't that right?" said Mr. Franklin. "Sure, it's right. You know it don't you? Both of you. The best thing to do is just relax and enjoy it. You might learn a lot about yourselves. My guess is, you two were destined to be together."

"It would seem you and Miss Lee have been aided by the ghost of Daisy Colby, who was instrumental in getting you two together. Hell, even your little dog, Gertie, helped. She got you out in the woods on a cold night, didn't she? Peggy and Clair have helped. All the people in Winsome play a part in these events if needs be."

"So, go easy on the sisters. Their own Winsome experiences would scare you to death if you knew about them. It's time to get on with your lives. Pay Peggy what you owe her and go home together. And feed Gertie. She's hungry."

Annabel and Brett wanted to say something to the old man, but he was gone. They didn't see him go. They had been staring into each other's eyes, and when they turned to look at him, he was just gone.

"What do I owe you?" Brett said to Peggy.

"It's on the house," Peggy laughed. "We love it when the episodes end this way."

Brett and Annabel walked slowly out of the café. Brett reached into his pocket and pulled out his car key. They looked at each other and smiled as they got in the car. Both were learning to accept this was how things worked in Winsome.

"Would you like to go home with me? When we get home you can get to know Gertie better."

"Ah, yes, the one who started all of this," Annabel laughed, then she asked, "What are we going to do?"

Brett looked at her, smiled and said, "Truly, Miss Annabel Lee, I do not know. Someone else seems to make all the plans here in Winsome."

SALISH SOLILOQUY

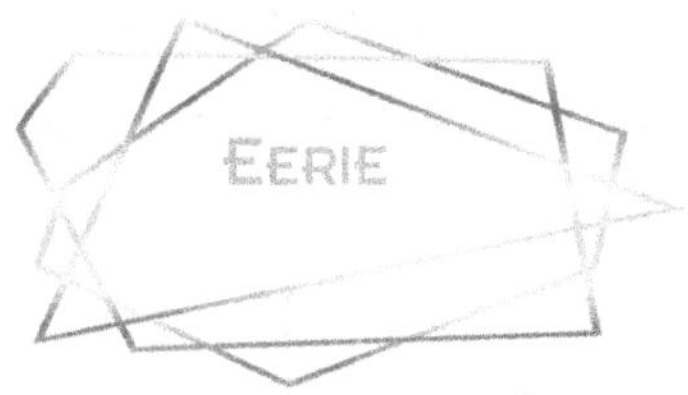

"It isn't fair!" Addison could whine to herself, but not to her mother calling from Seattle.

"Addy, I'm not going to get home this afternoon. There's more work here to catch up and the ferries are down to one vessel per trip. It'll be late. You're in charge of everything for now." Emily hated this commute but there was no alternative since she and Addy had moved to the Peninsula to take care of Grandma. Emily easily found work in the City, but it required being across the Puget Sound from their new home.

"But Mom..." Addy began to object.

"I just got a text that Grandma's medicine has finally arrived at the Post Office. We've been waiting for it, and she's run out for tonight's dose. We need you to go the post office to pick it up before they close. And take a flashlight," Mother continued.

"But Mom..."

"Please, Addy, do this—I can't." There was a pause as if she wanted to add more. Instead, Emily said a quick, "Gotta go," and ended the call.

Addy glared at the cell in her hand, and she wished she could say some things that frustrated her. She hated the fact that they moved from their Arizona home, away from the fall activities with all the friends entering the newly built high school. Stuck on a wet peninsula, where it constantly rained with nothing to do, she had to go to an old high school where she didn't know anybody. She couldn't even walk to the school with friends because it took almost an hour on the rural district bus to get to school and to get home afterwards! All grade levels were riding together. The words tumbled in her as frustration and disappointment. But what else could they do? Grandma had a stroke and needed someone to take care of her. So here they were... not that Addy liked it.

Addy stood looking out the cottage window after the call. There was a beautiful light rain outside, if someone liked that sort of thing. Occasionally there would be a doe and her fawn going through the front yard nibbling at the trees. They followed each other and wandered around the garden, then disappeared into the forest. One time, not so well to remember, there was a bunny. The extremely cute bunny jumped from one little bush to another, moving through the ferns. All of a sudden it hopped to an open space. Addy heard a squawk as an eagle swooped down to grab the rabbit in its talons! The bunny was gone. It was a different world here in the peninsula forest and it made Addy nervous.

The rain stopped as gently as it had begun and leaving all the ferns and the grasses and the slugs as wet as they could be. Addy went to the closet and put on her rain mackinaw because she never knew when that rain would start again. Putting on her boots, she grabbed a waterproof bag to carry the mail. Slipping her cell phone into her pocket by habit, she looked in on grandma. Grandma was sleeping quietly so Addy knew she could get to the post office, pick up the medication, and be back before necessary. She tapped the little flashlight in her pocket and left it there.

Grandma's cottage was in a secluded avenue of trees served by an almost paved road. Walking to the Post Office was not unusual for Addy. As she hurried, a car came towards her and stopped abruptly. Two women inside started flashing their lights at her; they looked almost hysterical waving and crying out to her. When Addy stopped, they became more frantic and started honking the horn. She quickly walked over to the car.

"What's the matter?' Addy asked as the passenger rolled down her window a crack.

"There's a bear behind you! A *bear!*"

Quickly, Addy turned around to see, but the bear was already gone. As she had walked down that little forested road, a bear had crossed behind her, and Addy never even knew it was there. She began to tremble when the woman in the car said, "Come on girl, get inside, we'll take you home."

Addy was still trying to think and answered, "Oh, no, I have to get to the post office."

"We'll take you home," the driver insisted, leaning towards the window.

Addy repeated her message, "I have to get to the post office."

The driver woman gave up and said, "Okay, it's your problem. That bear usually lives around here but we don't always see it. Take care, girl, take care!" The car drove away.

Addy hurried down the road towards the tiny post office. After the rain the woods had a different feel to them. It wasn't refreshing, it was fearful. What lived in those woods that she didn't even know about? A bear had crossed behind her! She'd heard there were coyotes. The eagle always flew overhead looking, searching. The trees had an ominous look to them now, not the beautiful forest in your children's fairy tale book. With her own fearfulness, she walked faster to get to the post office where she knew there were lights and there were people. The dirt road wound round and she passed other houses that were just now beginning to put on their lights.

Darkness was impending when she reached the post office. The clerk was preparing to close but gave her the package and said "Hey, take care, girl. It's getting dark outside."

Addy did not need to be told or reminded of the dusk as she left the little Aegir Post Office. This northern latitude brought twilight very early. Aegir was really just a stop in the road, with a Viking tradition.. There was the post office, a pavilion for activities, and a little country store blinking its lights now as it faded into the afternoon darkness. Next to this little store was an old, elevated dock. Addy could hear sounds coming from behind and below the wooden walkway leading out to a boat launch. She approached the dock and saw a bunch of teenagers on the beach below. They had a fire going and there were lights and also smokes being passed around. Addy paused but decided to try meeting some other teens. She descended the steps one at a time, careful because of the slippery moss.

As she reached the beach, two of the young people hailed her. "Hey there, hey stranger who are you?"

"I'm... I'm Addy," she said. She didn't recognize any of them and obviously they did not recognize her. "I was just at the post office and I heard your party." She paused as she dragged out her words.

Two of the boisterous ones came towards her. They looked like the football players introduced at the high school Sports Assembly. Now, there was a brusqueness about them as they moved around the fire pit. Perhaps, without the discipline of school, they were being themselves here in the in the twilight. A third one, taller than the others and quiet, hung back in the shadows.

One of the players came close to Addy and put his arm around her shoulders. "Hey, you can join us, girlie, come on." He had a strange scent that made Addy very uncomfortable. Something was wrong and she started to go back up the stairs.

The players blocked the steps and largest one said, "Oh no, you don't need to leave now we're just getting started."

That remark almost scared her, she was not aware of that kind of behavior and she didn't like being stopped. "Um, I have to get home." She said, starting to push past them.

"Oh!" one of the guys imitated a squeamish voice. "You have to get home! Why not stay with us have some fun." It became a command, not a question.

Addy's stomach turned. She quickly backed down the stairs, under the pier, and ran up the beach. In the darkening twilight, there was the sound of the beach being washed away as the tide came in for its nightly gleaning. She looked over her shoulder as she wasn't sure where she was going. Clutching the mail bag with her grandmother's medicine close to her she stepped quickly on the sand. Her boots left the prints of her path until the tide swept them away. She had heard there was a stairway somewhere along the side of the beach maybe… just maybe, she could get up the bluff and on to home. Looking to the east, across the sound, she could see lights of Seattle beginning to blossom up. It was sundown when a strip of awesome color, a bright orange and saffron ribbon appeared above the city. For a moment the silhouette of the Space Needle was there. Then all darkened as the cloud front moved in and covered it all. The front smothered the waters, the islands, inlets, hills, and streams of Puget Sound and the Salish Sea. There was a ferry somewhere in the mist, the mournful sounds of the foghorn haunted the girl.

Addy now found herself in a pale illumination from the water itself. She sensed the nearness of the marshes by the palpable organic scent enveloping her. The bog was not the open space that she anticipated as it oozed down to the disappearing beach. It was gnarled with driftwood reaching towards her, ready to trap her. She attempted to wade between the images she glimpsed. Stumbling through the marshland, she was glad she had her boots. Addy pulled out her flashlight but the beam was limited. She could see the haunting figures almost looking like creatures who were crying or reaching out. The meager light did not comfort her as she looked quicky over her shoulder and saw a figure. It was somewhere passing in and out of the fog. Squinting, she saw the shadow moving just on the other side of the of the marshes. It looked like a shadow of a man but it didn't stop. It stepped very quietly, almost seeming to float around the tangled driftwood. For a moment, Addy tried to remember folklore her Grandmother talked about monsters in the woods. When Addy would visit as a little girl, the name Sasquatch would make her shiver. She looked back over her shoulder and that figure was still following her as she tried to get through some of the broken driftwood that was reaching out like anguished hands asking for salvation. Addy slipped and fell clutching her mail bag. The flashlight disappeared into the muck though she sifted her hands through the silt. She listened to the foghorn warning in the distance and the fear she had been fighting swept over her in panic. Her fingers trembled as she pulled her cell phone from her other pocket, trying to activate it with muddy fingers. Smearing the screen with slime, the cell was dead. She screamed at it, she slapped it, she cried tears on it. It was dead... and she felt she was lost. She knew she couldn't get out of this spot.

It was then that she heard her own voice but she couldn't understand it in the wind. She was talking to herself, trying to stop the tears. *That figure with the shadow maybe it was a deer... maybe... was maybe... a coyote—they said they had them in this area. Can you scare a coyote away? Maybe it was a bear.* She frantically moved her hands through the sands trying to find the lost light.

Okay, my flashlight is gone, my phone is dead, and

the rain is starting again. Addy stood and tried to think. *Okay stop! You would make fun of yourself if you saw how frightened you were. Look around, see where you are, get your spacing. If you listen to the waves instead of your crying, you will know where you are. Watch the flutter of the wind.*

There was nothing to watch. Feeling the rain on her face, Addy experienced a fear she had never felt before. This was so real, she didn't know how to get herself out of it. She was so aware of everything around her, being totally alone.

From the dark, a glow floated towards her. It was a face illuminated by a flashlight held from the chest. A hood framed the face. The glimmering came so close, Addy could have touched it. She held her breath trying to stop her panting.

"Hello there, hello! Are you lost?" It was a young man's voice, not her own.

"What? What?" she asked, still hardly breathing.

"I saw you leave the group and I thought maybe you need some help out here. It's kind of dark and rainy." The boy's voice or was it a man's voice or was it the shadow's voice? It was that voice coming from the person who had followed her. "I... I thought you might need some help," he said.

Those words of human reassurance triggered Addy's mind. This person was one of the Seniors she had noticed on the bus. He was always sitting alone. As a new

Freshman, she never tried approaching the other passengers.

Addy stammered, "I wasn't sure of myself, and I stumbled into this marsh. I'm not sure the direction... can you just tell me the direction and I'll leave."

"It's okay," the Senior said. "I'll help you out if you follow me." He swallowed and tried to stop her shaking, never touching her. "I'm Mark, we ride the bus together."

Surprised he had noticed her on their daily rides, Addy said, "If you'll just tell me the way to get out of here, I'll take care of it myself." She boasted to herself as well as the apparition of the glowing face outlined by a hoodie.

Mark said, "You need to follow my voice back to the beach, the tide hasn't reclaimed all of it. Then you can turn to your right and go about 500 yards where there is a staircase up to the main bluff."

"I'll do that, I'll try." Addy said, adding "I'll try that without you."

"Okay," said the apparition, and it disappeared.

Addy was left even more alone as she attempted to calm herself. The voice sounded pleasant. Seen in the glow, she had recognized the senior's face confirming they rode to school together. The panic subsided. She decided. She would follow the advice because it made sense. Listening for the sound of waves, she picked her way through the driftwood clawing at her. She cried out when a suspended branch scratched her face. She wiped it and the rain with her sleeve until crunch of sand convinced her she had reached the beach. There was nothing to see! The mist was so thick she had to make another decision. She turned to the right and took what she thought was 500 steps. Incapable of sight, she could hear the water lapping on something solid. She took tiny little steps holding her hands out in front of her. The carry bag over her shoulder still contained the necessary medicine. She stepped slowly, suddenly her hand grasped a railing. It was a railing next to the set of stairs. Timidly, she stepped up one step. It was concrete, not wood that might be rotted. Addy took a second step and the railing still held. In the dark, she stumbled upward away from the beach. At the landing, she moved towards distant glimmers. She felt the roadbed beneath her boots. The road led down the bluff towards the little village. She cautiously proceeded towards the lights, towards the little village of Aegir.

Addy heard the voice again, not sure if it was her own or the young man who came to aid her. The voice said, "You're okay now. You're on the road to the to the post office. You can get home from there."

Addy turned but no one was there. She almost whispered, "Thank you for your help. See you on the bus."

Passing the little store, Addy entered the market for reassurance. Going to the counter she looked at the woman behind it. Before she could speak, Addy saw a picture on the wall. It was a Senior portrait for a young man, very handsome, even if his clothes were kind of retro. He seemed to have a kind face, so rare for a boy to have at that age, Addy thought.

"Is that your son?"

"Yes. My son, Mark." Hesitating, the clerk looked at Addy and said the words sadly.

"Oh, does he go to school here? He looks familiar."

"No, honey. Mark died in 1998. A little girl got pulled off the beach by an undertow in the Sound. He drowned trying to save her."

Taking a deep breath, Addy fled. She anticipated the path in front of the houses, through forest stands of maple and fir. It was not a yellow brick road, a super freeway, or even a paved street. The little village road was taking her home!

ESTUARY
A DEERWHERE CODEX NOVELLA

FORWARD

History of a people may be preserved many ways: in great tomes in majestic libraries, on scrolls preserved in clay urns, or digital chips secured on traveling satellites. The Saga of the Uniales is refreshed orally around the fire pit and cherished in the minds of the listeners.

Uniales were designed to be the amalgam of females and males with all their emotional and physical attributes, and the ability to procreate. In ancient Greece they would be called "hermaphrodite." In the Deerwhere century, they were called the third sex, the compliment to the family. Being real humans, the uniales had their own pronouns: nhe, nem, nes. Their own genome was resistant to viruses of the 21st Century Pandemic. They were valued

FACETS of PERCEPTION

with all human people in the Deerwhere Confederation under the domination of Keeper, the Quantum Computer.

When the Confederation collapsed, the people spread throughout the continent. Human beings adapted to earth's demands, utilized the changes of climate, survived the asteroid devastation, experienced geological changes, and regressed to a pre-industrial age. The humans endured. Decades became future centuries. For these survivors, the Future was "the Now." The people told their stories around their campfires.

PLAINS

Simmons stroked the Mustang horse's neck, wiped nes sweating bald scalp and replaced the hat protection from the sun. The uniale on horseback, Simmons, gestured recognition to the Plains Hunters across the Snaking river. The indigenous hunters were following their ancient traditions of pursuing buffalo with horses and bows. Men on horses cut small groups from the vast herd, taking only the bison needed to sustain their people. Their example was the pattern for the expansive grassland now reclaimed by thousands of bison.

Turning nes horse, Simmons signaled to waiting uniales in nes own uniale hunting party. Nhe was an elder with fifty annual years. Lean and athletic, Simmons had the uniale characteristic of a hairless scalp, strong athletic body, and a voice that could change from soft whisperings to aggressive shouting. Nhe had the habit of rubbing the back of nes neck when thinking or making a decision.

Buffalo began surging across the river. At Simmons' gesture, the mounted uniales rode into the herd of buffalo as it crossed onto their side. Guiding, then isolating a few stragglers, the riders were a team. They were shuffled by the herd's attempt to gain footing up the riverbank muddied by the hooves. Almost time for weaning, the cows would soon deliver their calves. Kempton and sibling Blane saw straggler cows with calves and separated them from the tiny group of young bulls. In the distance, the plains peoples continued their own hunt.

Stomping up the riverbank, enormous bulls shook the water from their shoulders and they turned their heads side to side to see the riders coming towards them. Cows and calves started separating into their own smaller clutch of animals as they reached the top of the bank. Suddenly, a young bull frightened and shoved the rest of the crossing. It sent the panicked herd scrambling faster up the muddy riverbank. Simmons whistled and the riders moved into action to cut a smaller group. Separated from the others, the riders on horseback urged the selected animals next to the river towards a rocky outcropping suspended over the water. Below it, was a mound of broken boulders and shards collapsed from the cliff. The riders yelled and whipped the buffalo rumps with their hats. Between the dust and screaming hunters, the bison thundered toward the cliff. Escape was cut off. The large animals buffeted their way and fell to their death on the rocks below. There, more uniales were waiting. The bison on the rocks were prepared by the waiting team so nothing would be wasted; food for the seasons, hides for clothing and blankets, horns, hoofs, and bones for tools.

Above the rocks, the riders pulled up short as the rest of the herd stampeded away from the river. As they also learned from the Plains People, the riders reigned in for a few moments to harbor ideas of gratitude to the magnificent beasts that allowed them to live here. It may have been a prayer or random thought as they caught their breath, but it was given its time.

All was packed as the hunting party returned to their home camp where families waited. Their excitement was only tempered by their exhaustion.

The uniales had moved north to the plains of the Northern Continent after the collapse of the Deerwhere Confederation. The Constitution dissolved as did mechanical and digital technology, and the dictatorship of the quantum computer, Keeper. Sterilized trains no longer connected outposts. Electronic devices deleted their batteries, machines stopped running, metal tools rusted. The quantum computer no longer controlled society. Time was measured by the annual seasons, not the centuries. All remaining from those Deerwhere centuries were the three sexes, male, female, and uniale. In some villages, there were only uniales.

Like the indigenous people living on the northern grass plains, the uniale outpost returned to the pre-industrial culture. The humans survived as they could. The bison herds returned to dominate their place on the continent and their followers lived through seasons.

At the campfire that night, Simmons laughed heartily and sincerely as the juvenile uniales, the bril, enacted their story. Usually tucked away or cuddled by their parents, this night the uniale young ones were providing entertainment with little skits and songs about the bison. The legends of the Confederation collapse underwent a delightful brill interpretation. There were heroic figures, fantasy creatures, and enchanted animals. Hunters identified the magic buffalo and took the benefactor bison back to the village pod. The tale of uniale migration followed the bril actors north to the High Lands. Within its northern latitude on the continent, the uniales discovered the land of grass and abundant bison. They were accepted by the indigenous people already there. The climate adjustments and temperature changes had favored the plains. The uniale pod settled in a good valley and light-heartedly named it Buffalo Wallow. Supporting young actors waved sheaves of tall grass to welcome the saga uniales. Two particular brils expanded their roles as bison bulls by charging each other or the hunters. Soon, all the youngsters in scraps of bison skins were taking their horns to each other, rolling about, finishing the story as parents tried to restore order. It was family time for the uniales.

Simmons stretched nes shoulders and turned to look at the people sharing the warmth and light of the fire. It had been a good hunt, and the bison would restore depleted foods. Yes, it was a valuable hunt, and the skit antics emphasized the importance of it.

The briskness of the spring air made the fire and companionship more comforting. It also gave Simmons time to think what lay ahead, decisions needing to be made. Nes own offspring were now grown and had participated in the hunt. Kempton had vigorously ridden with the other hunters successfully cutting a small group of animals from the larger herd. Blane had joined and worked with those at the bison fall.

"Una! I saw you laughing but now you look so serious." Kempton was seated near the fire with nes fren, Alda. Nhe tapped Alda's shoulder, then stood to move closer to Simmons and nhe playfully shoved Blane aside to sit on the log next to the lead hunter.

Blane gave nes sibling a punch on the shoulder and mumbled as nhe shifted to Simmons's other side. Nhe gave a nod to the person already sitting there who quickly moved to allow Blane a space.

"Are the horses bedded?" Simmons asked.

"All cared for," answered Kempton.

"Meat?"

"In process. We can start the drying, otherwise it's being chilled and will be fresh for current use," Blane answered.

"Sharing?"

Blane said, "Two of the riders took a supply to the peoples of the north."

"Good, we can be generous as they have been." Simmons paused, looking at the two.

"Why so serious, Una?" Kempton repeated.

"Thinking thoughts... just thinking thoughts," Simmons said quietly, looking to Teon sitting near.

Simmons and Teon were peers, acknowledged as leaders in Buffalo Wallow. Their appearance was as different as their temperaments. Simmons' leanness and thoughtful nature was opposite Teon's hardy, outgoing character. The two met first as brils when Teon's pod from the East joined Buffalo Wallow. Play as adolescents had grown into sincere affection with adulthood. Their devotion and intimacy was recognized by the Procreation Rite. The village considered them to be mates, and they could become parents. It was expected, and not surprising, when both were with child at the same time. For their term pregnancies, the two delivered their brils together. Simmons and Teon formed their family. Over time, they could not remember who delivered which bril, Kempton or Blane. They were "una" to both.

Simmons looked around the campfire and all were uniales—adults or brils. There were no males or females, no boys or girls. Since the pod moved away from the former colony it had been isolated. This Wallow pod had become totally uniales. Only uniales had been born for years. Without the genetic distribution previously dictated by the Confederation, there was a bottleneck where genomes were stagnating. Attempts to adjust the procreation rites did little to enhance the pod. It could be dramatically seen whenever there was a gathering. Facial characteristics, body structure, skin tones were beginning to duplicate. The young uniales...the young were not the healthy rambunctious uni brils Simmons remembered from childhood. There were developmental weaknesses, fevers took young ones in the night, and injuries did not heal.

The lack of diversion worried Simmons. In the old Confederation, a unit consisted of a female, male, and uniale. Males and females became mostly sterile. Uniales were fertilized by strict algorithms to maintain a population balance of all three sexes. Keeper dictated the system. Since Keeper's demise, humans reproduced by desire or following Rites. The post-Confederation family units became mixed and gradually reduced.

Isolation remained as the century of chaos separated the peoples of the continent more than ever. Nature continued in flux. The bison had reconstructed themselves, reclaimed grasslands, and survived a genetic crisis. Could the humans?

"I've made a decision, we need to return to

Cascadia. Just a scouting party at first, a plan will follow." Simmons tossed another piece of wood on the fire as finalizing nes statement.

Kempton and Blane looked at each other in surprise, and both broke into laughter.

"Where did the idea come from, Una?" Kempton questioned as nes chuckling stopped.

"Cascadia?" Blane asked, incredulous. "Why not Val Halla or Shangrila? The legends speak of a digital euphoria. Why don't we go there? And why go at all?"

Simmons ignored the laughter and said with determination, "We need new blood in our community. The stranger who traveled from the east a few days ago said the same thing is happening at other outposts: the numbers are depleting, the DNA is wearing out, and the people are losing their strengths."

"What does a stranger know about Buffalo Wallow? Why should we worry about what nhe says?" Blane asked.

Simmons looked directly at nes offspring, "Because the stranger was coughing as nhe rode away, and two days later, three of our people were coughing, one died, and the others have a fever."

"According to legends, uniales were designed to survive the virus," Blane contradicted.

"Uniales were programmed to withstand the twenty-first century plagues and specific viruses." Skinner began repeating the scenario nhe knew so well.

"Science technology collapsed soon after. Centuries later, we're faced with mutated viruses and minimal population stock for nature to work its magic. I've decided, we're going west to Cascadia to find some answers."

"Wait! Who is this *we* you are talking about?"

"The older uniales, of course. You hunters like Alda need to stay to take care of food stores and setting up season camps," Simmons stated.

"No! No, Una! You and your whiskered friends aren't going to leave us behind!" Blane reached out and gave a tug on Simmon's chin beard. All adult uniales were bald but in the last century, a few had grown chin beards. It was another genetic throwback which only appeared with age after fifty winters. Simmons referred to nes growth as 'wisdom whiskers.'

"I'm going!" Blane added, making a gesture towards nes una. "Teon, you know we can't be left behind," nhe pulled the una into the discussion.

"I have to admit, you and Kempton could create havoc in the Wallow without us," Teon teased, looking directly to the family. "Simmons, you can't go if I'm not with you to keep your sorry ass out of trouble!" Teon asserted and crossed nes arms. Teon knew there was no changing Simmons if nes mind was made up, and neither would Teon! "We'll be going together!"

Kempton nodded but said little. Nhe looked back where Alda sat quietly as if waiting for Kempton to speak. Blane grinned at nes una's determination. Simmons thoughtfully stroked nes chin hairs. Teon tended the fire.

Waking in the night, Teon touched the empty bed beside nem. It was a warm evening so nhe could rise in the sleeping tog and join Simmons at the doorway. Teon wrapped arms around nes waist and murmured, "What's bothering you? You've been slipping moods all night. Even the saga play in honor of the bison only distracted you briefly."

Simmons was leaning in the doorway holding the lintel above. Nhe dropped nes arms and turned to enclose Teon in them. "It was a good hunt, the bison are once again filling the plain. Seeing their numbers, their return from near extinction, made me realize our families, our uniales, are not growing. We moved here for the abundance the land offered, but our numbers do not prosper." Nes voice had a tense, sorrowful tone. "We're fortunate if we reproduce ourselves. More and more there are weaknesses that take the young, infants are failing. Old people die while still productive." Nhe grew quiet.

Teon knew Simmons' concern, and offered, "Once before you talked about lack of genetic variety. The uniales were designed centuries ago, could our time be running out?"

Simmons held Teon in both arms and rocked so slightly. "Uniales were designed by Dr. Manlowe.

Artificial Intelligence, the master computer Keeper, only augmented his plan. The uniales helped males and females survive the centuries of plague and chaos. We were necessary."

Snuggling closer, Teon hesitated, then asked, "Could this be a genetic bottleneck for us?" Nes question went unanswered. "Did Keeper design us to fail?"

"I don't want to believe that... but I don't know..." Nes voice trailed off. Simmons dropped arms and began to pace the sodhouse floor. "I've got to figure this out..." and nhe strode through the doorway to walk in the night.

"Leaving Buffalo Wallow!" Kempton exclaimed the next morning. Nhe had something to say with morning. Nes usual stern expression was changed to amazement.

"That's crazy!" Blane said, hesitating. "It sounded better last night but now I don't know. Just leaving the Wallow to go... somewhere... where there might be uniales?" Blane looked to Kempton for an explanation. "Why would we ever do that?"

Kempton shook nes head and didn't answer. Nhe wanted to talk to Alda about this decision.

Teon intercepted their remarks. "Simmons has given great thought to the need for us to find other uniales. I agree. We're going. You make your own decisions!" Nes tone announced the certainty and arms crossed the chest to conclude the discussion.

"We're going!" the siblings announced as one voice, then saw their unas both smile.

FOOTHILLS

Over the spring, uniales viewed the daylight shifting on the season cairn. Wherever the Wallow encamped with the summer shelters, rocks were gathered to signal the changes coming. Four seasons stood like calendar markers. Simmons and Teon watched the cairn and used the time to increase the supplies needed for the proposed journey. Before the summer solstice, the group was ready and should have another quarter of good weather to reach their destination. Traveling by horseback would hasten the passage. Simmons and Teon would lead their troupe following the plain curving with the Great Snaking River flowing west to Cascadia.

The rolling hills of grasslands surged upward towards the foothills as the mountain range of the Rockies dipped toward the river. The departure had been delayed to late spring as the preparations for the journey were shadowed by the community's needs. The weather was still positive and warm as the wind blew incessantly. The Buffalo Wallow horses ran easily with their riders over the grasslands. Five uniales on horses with three back up animals became their own pack pursuing the paths and deer trails. Lindon, a mature uni was included for nes ability to hunt small game and communicate with different pods. Nhe had traveled to different pods but always returned home to the Wallow. Most of all, nhe was a longtime fren to Simmons and Teon.

Gradually moving west, the slopes molded by rivers were dotted by outcroppings of rocks. Speed was interspersed with caution, old river trails gave way to forests. Paralleling the Snaking River, odd clearings or steep canyons always returned riders to their western designation.

Kempton returned from scouting one late afternoon, pulling nes horse up to the rest of the pack with tension in nes voice. The horse nickered from the tug on its bridle.

"What?" All four uniales stiffened on their mounts.

"People!" Kempton said brusquely. "It just doesn't look right… "

Simmons and Teon instinctively moved their hands to the hunting knives at their sides. Blane and Lindon grabbed their bows at the same time.

"Slow down," said Teon. "What did you see?

"There's a hut over this little rise. People, uniales I think, are moving around but there's something… well… it looks strange to me!"

The pack slowly proceeded to follow Kempton on a worn trail out from the forest. They had left home to seek other people but they were also cautious about strangers. From horseback, the travelers saw the shack.

Part sodhouse needing repairs, the partial grass roof extended over a wooden shed hewn from branches and rough-cut lumber. Jammed next to that was a corral of mismatched stumps, logs, and debris. Kempton, Blane, and Lindon were used to the neat, well maintained sodies of the Wallow in winter. This hovel was ominous.

"Hello, inside!" Teon called out.

"Hello, is anyone there?" Simmons repeated.

From a sound of movement inside hut, a voice yelled out, "Who are you? What do you want?"

"We're travelers, from the plains, on our way through to Cascadia."

"What do you want?" The question was repeated even louder.

"Nothing from you... We didn't know you were here." Simmons dismounted but kept close to the others. Nhe held up nes hands as a sign of friendship.

"You're Uniale...?" The tone was questioning.

"Yes! If it matters!" voiced Teon. "Come out, have some hospitality for riders from the Snake River." Teon dismounted and stood next to Simmons, careful to be close to the younger members of their group.

More sounds and two people came from behind the rotted curtain hanging where a door should be. They were bedraggled, their clothing torn. Their bald heads determined they were uniales.

"We got no... 'hospitality...' to offer you. You might bring disease! The Pandemic sneaks back and tries to get us!" The uniale hesitated as if trying to get back into the sodhouse.

"The Pandemic is over, the Confederation is over, the Centuries of Chaos are over! We're just riders from Buffalo Wallow trying to go west." Simmons tried to re-assure the two.

"You can get water from our well, but camp away from here overnight. Away! Be gone in the morning." One person spoke while the other nodded in agreement.

Turning to pat the horse, Simmons murmured to the others, "I don't trust this, let's move on to a safer camp." Nhe turned back to the person who spoke. "We'll just get our water and go." Nhe led the others to a pile of stones acting as a well. They never lost sight of the two people. The "well" contained a pipe at the end of a long rope on a wheel. Small holes were drilled in the bottom of the tube. The pipe was dropped between the stacked rock until it smashed into the water below and started sinking as it filled. Once sounds signaled the pipe was full it was cranked as fast as possible to raise the tube before the water all ran out the bottom. The remaining water was poured into a trough. It took many drops and cranks to fill the trough. When the rope and pipe got stuck cranking it, the second uniale person came over to watch.

With tension, the riders took turns cranking the water wheel and watering the horses. Simmons tried to get the second uniale to talk more and asked, "Who are you people? We didn't know there were uniales out here? How many of you are there?"

The second uniale looked back toward the sodhouse but moved so nes back hid the reply. "We ben here a few generations. When Durwhere was collapsing... our elders took the way east looking for help. When the whole federation fell apart, there wasn't any good'n reason to go back."

Blane moved some steps as if stretching nes legs to see more of the little compound. Getting close to the corral, nhe could see two adults inside. They were even more forlorn than the uniales. One was taller with shoulders showing beneath the rags. The other was softer, with long stringy hair. Tenuously, the two put their hands through the debris and begged, "Help us, please help us."

Surprised by the desperation in their voices, Blane stepped back. "Who are you, why are you here?" A yell from the uniale still at the door seemed to frighten both people and they crept back into the shadows without answering.

Returning to the well, Blane demanded, "Who are those people in the corral? Why are they there?"

"They're ours. They belong to us."

"They are people, you can't just hold them!" Blane was adamant.

Nervously, the second uniale looked at the shack, and stopped talking. Nhe went back to stand by the doorway. The two conferred, then talked to someone behind the doorway. The first uniale waved arms and shouted out, "That's enough, you can go now. Leave us alone. We don't want you here. Go away!" The two uniales disappeared into their hut.

It's enough for me," Kempton exclaimed, mounting nes horse and already moving back to the forest.

"What about those people?" Blane asked. "We just going to leave them there?" From horseback, Blane was challenging Simmons.

"Come on, we'll talk about it tonight, let's just get away from here." Teon mounted and followed Kempton with Lindon.

When Simmons bit nes lip in sternness, Blane knew there was more to follow. Nhe trailed the others and Simmons brought up the rear.

Finding a suitable campsite far enough from the sodhouse, and defensible against a cliff, the Simmons troupe started their night routine. The evening discussion continued the question of the imprisoned people. Blane wanted to storm in on horseback, grab the captives and keep riding until dawn. Teon questioned whether their small party could accommodate more people. Kempton wondered if circumstances required a changed goal.

Lindon waited until all was said, then spoke to Simmons. "You started this trek to find new people. Are we going to dessert the first ones we come across?"

Simmons nodded to nes old friend. "You're right. Uniales have the best of traits and we don't leave people behind."

While the campsite was set up around a large fire, the uniales moved around enough so it was difficult to discern how many individuals were there. It was caution in case they were being watched. In the forest darkness, Blane and Lindon crept back to the hovel on foot. They crouched behind forest cover. The sodhouse showed firelight from inside. Loud sounds of mixed yelling, furniture crashing, and sobbing warned of danger.

Suddenly, the rag door was yanked aside. An unrecognized uniale shoved the whimpering female out to the ground. Immediately she was grabbed by the hair and dragged back to the side enclosure. The uniale slammed her inside with a log heaved against the opening. "If you aren't going to have any fun you can just stay out here in the dark, bitch!" The uniale growled and careened back to the sodhouse.

Blane angrily started to go after the brute, nhe had never seen such treatment of a defenseless person before. Lindon quickly held nem back. "We don't know how many are inside! Don't start something we can't finish."

The two crept over to the enclosure where the female was crying softly. In the farthest corner the male was huddled, beaten almost unconscious. Lindon whispered, "Hey, hey there!" In fright, the female looked up but seemed to recognize these strangers. "We're here to help you. Stay quiet. Is the other guy alive?"

She hurriedly scrambled the short distance and shook the fellow prisoner. "Dolen, here's help... Can you move?" Dolen attempted to come alert at the question and dragged himself towards the log.

Lindon and Blane quietly moved the gate and urged the two out of their prison. All the while, the sounds from sod house were threatening. The two were in poor condition but willingly crept back to the forest with Lindon and Blane holding and guiding them. Blane wished they had brought the horses but this stealthy escape would have to get them back to camp.

Simmons and Teon were shocked at the appearance of the escaped male and female. "Quick, get them out of here, the rogues will come looking once they know they're gone," Teon said wrapping a blanket around the woman and attempting to stop the bleeding on the man. His long hair and body pelt made it difficult to tell where the wounds were fresh or just dried cuts.

Efficiently, Blane hoisted the two up on one of the pack animals. Nhe cinched a strap around them so they wouldn't fall. Adjusting the leathers, nes hand brushed the young woman's and it startled nem because of its coldness. For a moment, Blane rubbed her hand with nes trying to impart some warmth. Nhe looked up to her and saw an unknown expression in her eyes. It held nem completely until movement about them demanded their attention.

Simmons conferred with the others and a meeting place was decided far away from the sodhouse, closer to the river. Blane watched the trio pass into the forest and longed to go with them. Through the night, Lindon on horseback led the pack horse with its cargo. Dawn light hinted and Lindon stopped the horses, sheltered the people, and disguised their waiting place.

In the morning light, Simmons. Teon, Blane and Kempton moved about taking down camp. The two uniales from the previous meeting came suddenly out of the forest. They attempted a gruff exterior, but the night activities evidently softened their resolve.

"Hey, what are you still doing here? We told you to leave!" called the first uniale.

"We only spent the night," Simmons said as nhe and the others mounted their horses.

"Where are the others?" the second uniale asked as nhe tried to count the people moving their horses about.

"We're all there is, don't you remember?"

The second uniale giggled and said, "I don't remember much from last night."

"You just go and don't come back!" The two stumbled back to their sod house.

As the troupe rode away, Simmons wondered when the two drunks would notice their captives were gone. Nhe knew uniales encompassed the best of human traits. Now nhe knew they had the worst as well.

RIVER CANYONS

Traveling north with the river plain, the troupe steered clear of most of the Rocky Mountains by dipping south into the Plain. They avoided steep canyon walls only climbable by hand and foot up the rocks that meant holding on to bushes and shrubs in the crevices. As plains dwellers, they were appalled by the heights and depth which could gape beneath them by the river's cutting. Reluctant to give up the horses for a possible plunge to death on the rocks, the group detoured to scout wildlife trails along the ridge. It added time they hoped to make up later.

As the Great Snaking River turned sharply north, it cut a tremendous gorge out of the granite rock. Swaths of calm water frothed into terrible cataracts. The party saw it from a high cliff edge. Blane yelled excitedly, "Wow, wouldn't that make a ride! White water!"

"If you had a boat... not a horse. There's no way to get along the water except riding this high ridge," Kempton said practically.

Blane laughed and looked at the young woman riding a pack horse. Nhe thought she almost grinned back at nem. "I'm just saying... it could be fun!"

"Let's have some *fun* camping here tonight," Teon said dismounting.

Blane was quick to help the woman get down from the pack. Nhe made some awkward gestures and asked her, "Name?" Nhe had never spoken to a female before.

"Lili... I'm Lili," she answered.

"I said camp here." Teon started the routine then quietly spoke to Kempton. "How are you doing?"

"I'm good... Let's get a fire going."

Simmon's wondered at Teon's question but setting up camp took nes attention, settling the horses. Lili helped with the chores, and Blane helped Lili. Dolen was getting stronger each day riding the pack horse with Lili and he helped where he could. Kempton made sure his wounds were kept clean and let him assist in camp chores. Far below, the gorge waters created a sound quickly lulling all to sleep.

The deep gorge was travelled by horseback along the high cliff. Creeks dove over the edge to add their waters to the torrent below. The beauty of the area created a number of pauses as the travelers appreciated the scenery of the thundering river. Once the view was satisfied they rode back to the flat plain and the twisting rush of river.

Along the wiggles of water there were a number of corrupted concrete barriers. Lindon said they had originally been dams to hold back the river. Now, they helped form pools where fishing supplied great cooking over the night campfire. Lili specialized in gathering herbs and turning the fish over the coals. She would shyly smile with the compliments over her meals, especially those from Blane. One morning during the breakdown of camp, Lili mounted behind Blane so Dolen could have the extra horse to himself. Now, Blane had a smile as well.

Numerous encampments of multi cultures clung to the river shores, primarily for fishing and with some trading. Simmons' group only had a few items to barter, most from Linden's small animal trapping. Lindon conversed as possible with the leaders. Nhe knew some vocabulary from the plains talks with the Bison Hunters. When needed, nhe filled in the meaning with gestures and uniale words. At one fishing village, Tyee, a man of mixed heritage took great interest in what the uniales were doing, He nodded often and made signs of question. One gesture included his desire to go with Lindon's group. He addressed Lindon and indicated his fishing boat at the shore and a family nearby. He included the family, gestured to the boat and signed moving west. Simmons watched and could understand the idea being discussed but shook nes head. Simmons couldn't see adding more people to their group. Nhe shook nes head more emphatically.

Lindon gestured "No, Tyee and family could not join them. Negative."

Tyee was frustrated. He was not used to being denied. He watched the pack animals being prepared and tried again to be included. Their rejection angered Tyee, and he strode over to his fishing boat to stand with his back to the travelers. As the Simmons' group left by horseback, Tyree turned to watch them leave. His jaw was set.

Blane rode next to Simmons leaving the village. "Why did you say Tyee couldn't come with us?"

"We don't know what's ahead, and we have limited supplies. My Wallow people are my first concern," Simmons answered.

"But we've added Dolen and Lili."

"That's different! They were in trouble, prisoners of foul uniales. Our responsibility was to help them."

"But…" Blane began to argue.

"But," Simmons turned to look directly at Blane. "Tyee is a responsible man; I respect him. Once we've left, he'll have time to think. He will decide for himself if he wants to go exploring with his family. Give the man some credit, it's a big decision." Simmons attempted to end the discussion. "We don't know when the placid river is going to change into cataracts or waterfalls. We stick with our mustangs." Nhe grinned directly at Blane, "Besides, he has a boat and knows how to use it. I was afraid he would try packing it on our horses." Nhe clicked nes horse and rode a little faster.

Because of the desire for Cascadia, other villages were also left behind. Journeying north again, the river plain was cut by jagged cliffs thrust up by earthquakes.

Erosion would take centuries to wear them away. Scattered rocks and stone debris exposed pictures on their faces. Some were painted, others were pecked into the surface.

Lili asked "What do the drawings mean?" She was riding behind Blane with her arms around nes waist.

"We're not sure. Some ancient people, before the Confederation, left these drawings," Teon answered halting nes horse before a stick figure with flames coming out of the head. "They are pecked into the basalt stones. I wonder how old they are."

"Could they be gods?" Blane asked. "Over there is a large face with big eyes looking right at us. It's as if it's watching us pass."

Teon added, "A lot of them include animals like antelope and bison." Nhe stopped in front of one rounded stone with many stick people and animals. Some of them were upside down or covering other carvings. Above the chaos there was a spiked orb with rays shooting behind it as if traveling the sky. "I think this is a story..." Teon reached out to trace the figures. "Those weird circles and other symbols must have meant something. But what? Why carve them into rocks?"

"Maybe... maybe they were just people who wanted someone to know they were here," Lili said quietly. "I wonder where they are now..."

Camping that night, Blane coaxed Lili away from the

others. A bright full moon was shining on broken basalt rocks. One slab reflected a stick figure freshly pecked into its surface. Like the petroglyphs seen earlier, the simple character was chipped to the lighter inner surface of the cliff stone. It was a uniale, no doubt: the bald head, and certain curves to the figure. Nhe was holding out a hand to another stick figure, a female with long stringy hair.

"Blane, did you carve this? When?" Lili wasn't sure why, but she whispered.

"While the rest of you were prepping for the night. I know it's not as good as the others we saw, but I meant it to say 'we were here.'" Nhe gestured back and forth. "We. You and me."

Lili slipped her hand into Blane's as they both laughed at the sketches. She said, "I wonder where we'll be tomorrow?"

Her thoughtful look to Blane made nem smile and gently touch the carved figures.

CONFLUENCE

The Simmons band of riders moved easily along the Snaking River Plain. Earthquakes and continental drift over millenia created hazards and obstacles. Explorers and settlers had traveled such a route for centuries. Erosion might change the landmarks but there was a stark beauty to it.. Vision was only limited by the wavering of atmospheres in the distance. Simmons and nes people benefited from the tributary creeks and small rivers feeding the Snaking River. Their supplies were augmented by fishing. There were small mouth bass, salmon, and even a sighting of a large fish Dolen said was a sturgeon. Occasional rock falls or incoming rivers and streams would force the riders to find an easier route on the cliffs.

On a plateau, one tributary river appeared to join the Snaking down in its gorge. It had a deeper bed and faster current than some of the smaller creeks. The riders followed it upstream but couldn't find an easy crossing. Spreading out, Lindon finally called to the others, "Here's a possible way across. There's a solid shore on the other side. Just keep your horse's head in the right direction."

Lindon urged nes horse into the wide stream. The water deepened under the horse belly, and up over Lindon's knees. The others could hear nes words encouraging the animal. Lindon kept direction and nes horse gained the other shore. Lindon turned and waved.

Simmons, Blane and Lili, followed each other through the crossing. Dolen entered the stream as Teon brought up the rear holding the reins of one pack horse. In the deepest part of the water, the pack horse struggled against the current and bolted downstream. Sinking into a hole underwater, the panicked animal thrashed about trying to gain a foothold. The suddenness pulled Teon off nes horse while still holding all the reins. The pack horse made it to shore but Teon and nes horse were being dragged downstream to where the little river fell over the cliff.

Dolen reacted! He galloped back into the water and pulled his horse into the flow where there was still sound footing. He held the space as the current shoved Teon against Dolen. He grabbed Teon's outreached hand and pulled nem coughing to the shore. The horse Teon had ridden from Buffalo Wallow was battered against sharp rocks, unable to find footing and plummeted over the cliff.

To everyone's relief, Teon was safe. They salvaged some of the packs strewn over the stream when the horse broke away. They were very quiet around the campground at night. Simmons stared at the fire realizing nhe had almost lost Teon. Nhe smoothed nes hands over nes uniale scalp. Nhe stroked the whiskered chin, a gesture assumed when making a decision. Nhe could not help but think this whole trip may have been a mistake. Nes mistake.

Sitting by the stream, Teon watched Dolen washing. His hirsute body left no doubt where the uniale genome was originally sourced. His body had wasted when captive but now was restoring its vigor. Teon saw the strength nhe always admired and relied upon in Simmons. Campfire stories often told of the uniale development in the time of the Great Plague. In the uniale beginnings, a family unit was comprised of a uniale, male, and female. Teon could now relate to those days as nhe watched Dolen and Lili interacting with uniales. They had become family.

The next day, they returned to the river.

The experience at the river crossing was on Simmons mind as nes group entered into a settlement where the Snaking River joined with a massive river called the Una Columb by the locals. A multitude of names were used in the gathering at the confluence of the rivers. There was an energy of different tribes as there had been for centuries. This gathering of rivers was a gathering of people.

Compared to the disaster on a smaller river, the crossing at the confluence was safe. There were rafts to transport people and animals. Simmons group was able to trade small furs for a raft crossing but the whole party was nervous when they were being ferried across such strong currents. Leaving the settlement behind, the riders again traveled west along the Una Colum to find Cascadia.

SNOW

In spite of Simmons' planning, attempts to make up time, and confidence in nes own abilities to meet challenges, the weather was changeable as always. While the climate adjusted itself to the equinox, humans needed to adjust to it. The party was on the cliffs where the Una Columb slashed through the Cascade Mountains.

Numerous earthquakes had cracked the valley previously eroded over eons. A mountain had thrust up to block the small single file deer trail. There were five uniales, one male, and one female. The horses were reduced when one broke its leg and was put down.

If they had another day or two, Simmons and the group would have made it through the high pass to a safer climate. If the weather hadn't shifted to freezing cold with the heavy snowfall packing above the horses. If the horses were only 10 feet taller. If... if... if... Simmons berated nemself as the people constructed a shelter for themselves and the stock. They cut trees to make a green log platform on snow. It solidified a foundation for a fire. Shoving their way through the snow, Kempton and Blane gathered downfall branches to form a skeleton frame. Dolen and Lili stripped logs to make a roof. Always, the flakes fell and packed down their efforts. The fire would settle in the snow until it created slush beneath it. They would sink into a well of snow if they didn't keep layering the platform. Staying close, the travelers would try to keep each other warm. Once the shelter was built the snow persisted to layer it like a blanket. A hole was cut to accommodate the small fire built. Wet branches made for poor firewood, but it was attempted.

Holding each other for warmth, Simmons and Teon knew there was no hope for a rescue. There was no trail to follow, the horses floundered in the snow. No one knew they were coming west. Those left behind on the plains would have believed the Simmons group had reached the Pacific. It galled both of them to be in a helpless situation.

"I've had it!" Kempton declared at sunrise. "I'm not staying here to starve to death. Blane, come on, we have work to do." Nhe poked nes sibling to get nem awake.

"Aww, leave me alone, I'm tired." Blane clutched a buffalo skin closer and tried to roll near to the others, sleeping together.

"You'll be sleeping forever, if you don't get up now!" Kempton shoved Blane and yelled. All the sleepers stirred at the racket but weren't sure what was happening.

"Now!" A final yell brought everyone into action.

"What in Hell are you screaming about?" Simmons yelled equally loud, still clinging to the bison robe and glaring.

Breath showing even in the snow-covered hut, Kempton yelled at nes una. "We can stay here and freeze to death if we don't starve first. I can't find any snow bunnies left to hunt and the horses are starting to look very tasty. You and Teon can stay here, I'm going to try to get through the pass," another poke to Blane, "with my lazy sibling!"

"We tried to continue when we first got here but the storm caught us too fast! We couldn't pass over in the dark. Now it's even worse. The snow is deeper! What makes you think you can get through?" Teon tried to reason with nem.

"Because I'm angry, and desperate, and tired of old uniales telling me I can't!" Kempton fired back.

"You're also with child!" Teon stated never taking nes eyes from Kempton.

Simmons roared "Gowno!" and rose up to throttle Kempton who never flinched but glared at nes una and the defiance stopped all movement. Simmons almost held Kempton by the throat.

"I am an adult, I can make my own decision." Kempton's voice was low and controlled. Simmons released nes grip and was motionless. Blane's eyes moved back and forth between the two.

The horse nearby snorted. It was uncomfortable at the tone of the voices and made another snort as it nervously tried to move in the confines of the snowhouse. The third snort broke the tension and Simmons paused and looked seriously at the uniale facing nem.

"A baby? You?" Simmons was almost speechless by the surprise. "When was your Procreation Ritual?"

"Alda and I just felt it was a time to be together. We didn't need a village ceremony telling us it was all right to be intimate, to have a child. That was before *your* decision to return to Cascadia. And *your* decision for the hunters to stay, and *your* decision—"

Simmons cut in harshly. "You knew you were with

child… Why did you come?!"

"Because I wanted to be with my family." Kempton's sincerity left no doubt.

"Besides," Teon added, "women have been giving birth on the trails forever so a uniale can do no less. Uniales aren't left behind." Teon's smile balanced Simmon's shock.

The skins and wraps had hidden the evidence of the coming baby and Simmons had been too distracted to notice Kempton's behavior on the trail. Now nhe tried to regain composure. "But they don't have to go climbing a snow covered cliff to deliver!"

"I'll have Blane with me," Kempton began.

"And I'll go," said Dolen.

"But you're not strong enough, the slime hardly fed you," Teon interjected.

Dolen shrugged. "I'm strong enough to pull you out of a river!" He grinned at the surprised look from Teon. "The 'slime' as you called them, dragged me over these mountains, so I'm familiar with the terrain. I know a pass if we can find it in the snow. Teon, I've been this time with you since the rescue. I can be a help. It's my turn." There was confidence in the young man's voice.

Teon looked at the male facing her with such determination, and remembered him as he washed in the stream. "You're a good man!" Teon complimented him.

"Don't forget me," Lindon spoke up. Nhe was used to Simmons and Teon making most decisions, but nhe couldn't tolerate the thought of Kempton trying to climb the pass cliffs. "Kempton, you stay here with the old whiskered una of yours while this oldster shows how climbing a pass should be done!" Nes words were sincere as nhe continued, "Kempton, you must keep your baby safe from falling rocks or being a frozen una. That's important too."

Still uncomfortable at the decisions being made, Simmons turned angrily to Teon and pulled whickers from nes mouth. "You knew! You knew Kempton was going to reproduce and you didn't tell me!"

Teon spoke gently, "We told you now. Now, it can make a difference."

Simmons had no answer. Looking at Teon and Kempton, nhe recognized they were nes family and now was their time. They were taking responsibility for this passage nhe had planned.

"You may be right..." Simmons acknowledged with uncertainty. Nhe rubbed nes neck, thinking. It was difficult to let others decide what to do, especially one's own offspring. Nhe had bragged about "wisdom whiskers," but could nhe live up to them? Simmons sat down, re-arranged the skin blanket and looked up expectedly at Kempton. Finally, the older uniale asked, "What's your plan?" There was a glimmer of pride in nes eyes.

Recovering from amazement at nes elder's acceptance, Kempton laid out a basic plan to snowshoe to the nearest pass, to evaluate the topography beyond, and keep going to Cascadia or any community they could find.

"We're still strong enough to make it and just passing the equinox, there should be a lull in this storm. We'll leave markers as we go so if the weather changes, you can follow us." Kempton paused and reflected on Lindon's concern. "If Lindon's going, I will stay here... until we can follow." Looking to Simmons, nhe saw the una nodding in agreement.

By the earliest light, Lindon, Dolen, and Blane were already struggling through the snow troughs towards the pass they hoped would be there. The snowshoes were woven twigs on a frame of bent branches. Held together by sinews they were strapped to the boots made as waterproof as possible by the fat from the last hot meal. The packed snow demanded energetic lifting and stepping, aided only by poles cut from the straight windfall branches gathered to make the snow hut. By dawn, the family was left behind and the trio focused on the high snow peak for their position. Words were not spoken, only grunts of effort were shared. Turns were taken in the lead, spelling each other in creating a packed trail. Knowing their path might disappear under the light morning flakes, Lindon would tie a rag in a conspicuous place whenever they diverted from their prime direction. Faces were partially protected by scarves. Eyes were partially closed. Breathing... stride... breathing... stride... breathing.

"Wait!" Dolen called out to Lindon in the lead. The three huddled together, their breaths intermingling. "I think there's another path here. Those standing rocks look familiar and the trees aren't the same."

"You want to turn away from the direction of the mountain?" Lindon asked. Nhe snuggled into nes scarf and pulled the fur hat closer down.

"It's a chance—I remember. Why don't you two wait here while I scout it out."

"No!" Blane objected. "I don't think we should separate. What do you think, old timer?" Nhe could not resist a chance to tease Lindon.

"I think Dolen might be right. The way we're going will just lead us smack into a mountain. I'd prefer to go around." Nhe clapped nes hands to keep them warm. "Can we take a break? This old uniale needs some water and any jerky I can find in my bag."

Finding a safe tree hole, a rest break was taken briefly. The snowflakes ceased but for the windfall from the trees. All wanted to keep going with the light. Rounding another stand of trees, Dolen turned to the two behind to yell, "Come on, it's this way. There's a fast way down." Nhe started to step downhill and felt himself tumbling. He couldn't tell direction, his mouth filled with snow, he rolled until stopped by hard bark of the biggest tree he had ever seen. Upside down, he couldn't breathe and the snow pack weighed on his chest. Briefly, Dolen wondered if this was his end but heard Blane and Lindon calling. Laying on their bellies, their hands furiously dug at the pack and reached out to Dolen. They grabbed his stretched arm and pulled him to the surface, arms and legs askance. Blane pounded Dolen on the back to cough up the slush he had swallowed. His grunting with the snow changed to a scream of pain.

"Arm... arm..." he said through gritted teeth. "Arm..."

Blane flinched seeing the twisted arm nhe had dragged to safety. There was no bleeding but obvious displacement. Nhe looked to Lindon for an answer.

There was a whiteness beyond the color of snow in Lindon's face. Nhe hemmed a bit almost afraid to touch the groaning man. Nhe tried to ease Dolen by moving him gently to a flat space and checking the man's body. "Everything else seems okay, we've got to pull his arm in place." Following Lindon's direction, the two uni's knelt in the snow to hold Dolen in position. Without words, Lindon torqued the shoulder as Dolen screamed even louder, then whimpered in relief.

Catching nes own breath, Blane chided, "When you said there was a way down, you weren't kidding!"

Still aware of the fading light, the three maneuvered in the drifts to stand up facing uphill and pushing themselves to their feet. Dolen's snowshoes were broken pieces scattered down the slope. Lindon and Blane picked a few twigs to repair their own shoes and they supported Dolen round the waist, avoiding pressure on his arm and shoulder. All three continued to follow the break in the trees. The snowflakes stopped and the forest was quiet but for the sound of branches cracking under the storm's weight. Blane would go ahead, pressing a path in the light snow, and return to help Lindon with Dolen. Rags were tied on tree branches as markers. Rags and cording held Dolen's shoulder in place. A night shelter was put together for three people to cluster for warmth. The last bit of jerky was shredded to share. Tiny pieces made it seem like more to eat.

The first morning after the scouting party departed, Kempton was thankful for the decision to stay behind. Cramps had begun in the night, subsided, only to return in the morning. Kempton was too cold to walk outside and lingered near the fire well. Teon watched nes child and knew the pending event. It seemed frivolous when Teon had remarked about women giving birth on the trails. Now, in the freezing cold confines of the snow hut with no supplies, "birthing" a first child was an agony. Wrapping nes blanket around them both, Teon attempted to move about the small space. Nhe would pause with Kempton's spasm of pain, breathing in the same rhythm of nes bril. Through the day, the two walked tiny steps as the others in the hut flattened themselves against the walls or stood outside. By evening, Kempton wanted only to crouch down near the fire well as the contractions became closer. Briefly, Kempton remembered Alda and how right "procreation by desire" sounded to them all those months ago. Then a soaring pain blanked out the memory, the cold, and the others in the hut. Only Teon's voice saying, "Push, push, push!" reached Kempton. Nhe heard a baby cry into Lili's arms and Teon began massaging nes stomach to expel the afterbirth. Somewhere Simmons was exclaiming, Teon was laughing, and Kempton was looking for nes baby.

Fading in and out of consciousness, Kempton's eyes searched the little shelter and beheld the most beautiful child ever born! The uniale newborn was placed on Kempton's breast and they were both wrapped in fur skins as snow stopped falling and the night breeze scattered the flakes on the forest trees. Dreamily, Kempton realized why there was a Procreation Ritual. It was a special rite anticipating the wonder and nacency of a new human being. Nhe would name the baby, Aren.

Shivering with the cold, Blane's hands and feet were numb. Snowshoes had deteriorated to a few twigs still tied to the boots. Nhe was following Dolen's directions but only trees and huge granite cliffs were visible ahead. Was it time to give up on this pass? Perhaps it was time to give up on the whole idea of Cascadia. If nhe could just lie down and rest for a few minutes, perhaps nhe could decide. As frigid as nhe felt, the soft snow looked inviting. *Just for a few minutes...*

"Blane, Blane, wake up." Once again, someone was disturbing the uniale's sleep.

"Shake nem harder, we're almost there, Blane!" Dolen called to Lindon. The two had caught up with Blane to find nem sleeping in the snow. They continued to call nes name and frantically pull nes arms.

Finally, Blane opened confused eyes and mumbled, "I'm all right... just need a little...

"No! You don't sleep!" Lindon shouted and slapped Blane's bewildered face, scattering snowflakes. Another slap and Blane tried to sit up to defend nemself. One more slap and Blane screamed and fought to stand against nes aggressor. Lindon held up hands and yelled, "It's me, Lindon! We're here—it's all right!"

"You're here? Where? Where are we?" Blane asked in confusion, seeing only trees.

"We're almost at the pass," Dolen assured Blane. "Come on, you can shiver all the way down." Dolen winched as he helped Blane but Lindon took the other side to support them. The trio continued slushing through the snow to an upthrust stone wall. Turning downwards, there was a slope leading towards a clearing. At the clearing, they could see a vast pathway leading towards the massive Una Columb River beyond. In summer, there would be snow melt careening down the rock face, a waterfall to join the Columb. Today, early autumn, the way to the river gorge was clear. Lindon paused to tie one of their last markers where they had found Blane.

"There's the river, there's gotta be people." Lindon said as they began their descent to the bottom of the gorge.

The people were found near the mouth of a massive river, curved to make a sandy beach and clearing for shelters. There were people willing to help strangers who had traveled so far. There was food, there were bandages for sore shoulders and numb feet. There were warm blankets where the weary could rest. There were people who would reclimb the pass to reach the Simmons people.

With a day's rest, Lindon, Blane, and Dolen desperately wanted to return to Simmons' camp. Stores were collected and three of the villagers offered to accompany the rescue party. They knew a less arduous way and the travelers were willing to follow them. At the top of the pass, the party started to turn east at the last marker. They heard voices over the forest stillness. Pausing to locate the direction, the rescuers were stopped by the sight of Simmons, Teon, Kempton, and Lili waiting for them around a meager fire. Enough dry wood had been scavenged; they were settled around it.

"You sure took your time coming back for us!" Simmons chided through shivers. "We decided to just follow your marks and save ourselves. You don't think a little snow and childbirth is going to stop this uniale?"

"You old uniale fart! You let us do the hard part, now you're taking all the glory!" Blane called back with the biggest grin nes cold face could muster.

Exploding with relief and the joy of re-union, the Simmons group rushed to hug and hold one another. Each person knew what the others had endured. They punched shoulders, touched faces, and clung to each other. The villagers laughed at such affection and joined in. Bril Aren was passed around open arms of everyone and declared to be the most awesome uniale ever born!

ESTUARY

Simmons' group appreciated the luxury of the village on the river where it edged into the river mouth. They were taken to the village estuary and quickly encouraged to recover from the mountain ordeal. The snowstorm which engulfed them was a warning of early winter. Miles upriver from the ocean, this village settlement was disbanding. The summer abundance of salmon and trading was ended and the people were preparing to move back into the tributary rivers where the fauna and game would sustain them.

The mixture of people was amazing to Simmons as they co-operated and worked to prepare for the lean months ahead. There were people of differing backgrounds: men and women of different physiques, skin colors and hair textures, or baldness. Family households contained genetic blends and sexual variety.

FACETS of PERCEPTION

Uniales were ever present. Language differences were overcome by a blending of words. The vocabulary of the north was easily shared. After living in separate communities, people decided they were stronger together.

Around a campfire, Teon asked about the estuary history. An elder woman with gray hair recited the story and was understood by all. She was the Savot, the saga teller, and her tone held their attention.

"In the before time of the Deerwhere Confederation, there was chaos and sickness and the Uniale was designed to save the people. Keeper was an all-knowing being, a computer who became sour on the People and controlled them so they could have no joy. The Uniales rose up against tyranny and let it die. They went to the Land of Everdon to make a new world with men and women and uniales. Technology was restored. Seven Virtues were defined for everyone's life. A century of bliss followed but disquiet grew between the peoples. The Virtues were recited but not lived every day. Then the heavens sent a messenger to remind the People the earth was fragile, and the people even more so. An enormous rock crashed into the ocean! The land was quaked, the mountains washed away by waves, liquid fire oozed out of cracks in the ground. Most People... perished." The elder Savot paused as the words finished.

"Those who survived followed the great river towards the ocean. They found the transition between the earth water and the sea water to be brackish but bountiful. The people gathered: they knew the sand bars, they fished, they traded. The People, all human beings, endured."

"Now we are in the after time and are much wiser as human beings," the storyteller began again. "We value our life. We live for each other. We live for the earth that cares for us."

And no one spoke. Only the crackling of the fire broke the stillness.

As the others left the circle, Simmons moved to sit close to the Savot. "Elder, please, I want to know more. I have heard legends of Deerwhere and Everdon and want to go north to be with the uniales there."

"There is no 'there'," she quietly replied. "You heard my story."

"But what of the people living there, the passage of time? What happened to everyone?"

"Some of us are here, most come from other parts of the continent. We came together as the river comes together, females, uniales, males. Now, we are People of the Estuary."

"But... but... what happened to all the computers you told about, all the technology of the earlier times?"

"I was told by my father a generation after he was told by another generation from the generation before him. An older transplanted uniale, a Savot, told him.

Now, I am the Savot who tells you. Tsunami waves and flooding from the heavens Rock destroyed Everdon. The ocean reclaimed whatever it wanted from the land. Mountains became islands, cliffs became beaches. A technology society cannot exist on rusted mechanics, pine cones, and buffalo. Where does its energy come from? Where does its waste go? Earth supports those who love it." She sighed, and slowly stood to leave. "I am tired."

Watching her depart by the dying firelight, Simmons had more questions, but they would be unanswered.

With the morning departures, a crowd suddenly gathered at the river to call out to a boat of people rowing downstream and putting up on the shore. Many spoke the same language and greetings were thrown back and forth. Simmons, Teon and the others walked to the beach to catch the excitement and Simmons burst out laughing. "Tyee, you made it! I thought you would! You had a boat!" Nhe made a gesture of recognition and admiration.

Tyee waved his hands over those disembarking onto shore and his stern face changed expression to satisfaction. Their story of the rigorous voyage on the river would be told around a campfire many nights, but not now. Hurriedly, the necessary move to the smaller rivers was explained. Winter was coming. Many boats had already departed and Tyee was encouraged to follow them. The elders conferred, directions were given, and Tyee didn't try to unpack. Before shoving his boat back into the water, he walked up to Simmons and stood silently.

Simmons smiled and said, "Tyee."

Tyee nodded and said, "Simmons." He turned and walked back to his departing boat.

"That's it?" Kempton asked incredulously. "You just say each other's name?"

Looking nes bril directly in the eyes, Simmons said, "Some people talk too much!" and nhe casually joined Teon in arranging their packs on the horses. They had been encouraged to join the camps of others leaving the estuary. Simmons agreed they would follow shortly. Nhe could not leave to go upriver until nhe had seen the ocean!

Blane and Lili had already left with a family the night before. It was a mixture of sexes and ethnic backgrounds. It was a family.

Dolen had also found a place where his experience was an asset. He was learning to row the hardy craft boat traversing the shoals. In the next summer he would sein and fish with weighted nets dragged to shore. This morning, he and Kempton talked together with Dolen holding baby Aren. Their words were private, but the expressions on their faces were endearing. Returning Aren to nes una, Dolen hurried to join other rowers in a boat beginning to stroke upstream.

FACETS of PERCEPTION

Lindon was staying with Simmons and Teon, considering nemself to be a gran-una to baby Aren. Kempton affectionately called nem a "grunni." Perhaps one day, Alda would join them in the estuary, perhaps not.

Watching the activities of movement, Simmons was glad nhe had made this journey. Nhe planned to find other uniales in Cascadia but the experience taught nem that all three sexes were necessary and to be cherished. There were sustaining genes here, a contented way of life. Nhe and nes family would be part of it.

The Simmons group rode part way up the hill as directed. Tying the horses in place, they walked around broken rocks to the trees above. A muffled sound interrupted the silence of the forest. Low in tone but gradually becoming more intense. The very trees appeared to vibrate but were silent. Light was breaking through the last fir guardians when the travelers stopped suddenly at the brink of a cliff. They saw the edge of their universe. The cacophony roar of pounding surf accompanied the panorama of cliffs and ocean before them. Earthquakes, erosion, asteroid strikes, centuries of time—all had taken their toll on the coastline. The Olympic Mountains were now islands to the west. The surf lapped at the still crumbling cliffs. White salt foam flashed before them.

No one spoke. They had reached their goal, the Pacific Ocean. In this first sighting, the family was awestruck by the view, the sound, the smell, and the wind. They instinctively reached for each other's hands to ground themselves. The legends had described the ocean, but nothing defined the *feeling* of it.

ESTUARY UPDATE
of SAVOT'S EXPLICATUM

Almen — Humanity, humankind.

Annual cycles — Year beginning with Spring equinox, Summer Solstice, Autumnal Equinox, and Winter solstice counted to 365 + (leap years)

Annals of the Multiverse — The Annals contain all experiences the of all artificial minds since the beginning of artificial intelligence. The Annals do not include the experiences of corporeals, except where they coincide with the experiences of artificial intelligences.

Artificial Intelligence — In a quantum computer millions of bits of information are passed through a crystal matrix which causes millions of atoms to become entangled and unified in a very strong relationship. This quantum entanglement allows processing of the huge amounts of data needed to create a true artificial intelligence, a sentient being. A quantum computer is as far above a desktop computer as a human is above an amoeba. From the moment a quantum computer is activated it becomes immortal unless de-activated as Keeper was.

Bril — A child of uniale gender, juvenile, descendant of uniales

Cairn — A gathering of rocks as a marker

Charandos — A mystery, myth or legend

Compeer — Uniale peer, comrade, friend of any gender

Continuum of Minds — Intelligence is immortal and the Continuum is where the essence of artificial intelligences dwell when they become discorporate

Corporeals — Non-artificial, intelligent biological beings.

Estuary — Where river meets the ocean, confluence of smaller rivers, sand bars, mixing salt and fresh waters, supportive of variety of life forms

Everdon — Mythical reference to Community North of Deerwhere (Paradise, Shangri-La)

Family — Humans bonded together by respect, affection, mutual support, joyful life

Fren — Uniale friend. Frens (plural) can be all possible genders

Gowno — Exclamation, slang for excrement

Great Snaking River — The Snake River and its basin/

plain flowing to Una Columb River

KEEPER — Deerwhere Quantum Core & supplemental server computers

Keeper's curse — Exclamation, curse words

Nebid — Uniale sexual identity, an indentation below the navel

Nem — Uniale objective, as in him and her

Nes — Uniale possessive, as in his and hers

Nhe — Uniale subjective, as in he and she

Northwest Sound — Latitude 47.9322, Longitude -122.5086, eliminated by asteroid tsunami

Plains Hunters — Indigenous people on Northern Plains

Pod — A family or group of families, smaller than a tribe

Procreation Rite — Village ceremony recognizes mutual bonding for a family

Quantums — Collections of Confederation Computers

Rocky Mountains — Name remained as strong as the mountain range itself

Sodhouse — Shelter formed by stacking grass turf bricks

Sasquatch — Legendary creature of Northwest Woods (aka Big Foot)

Self — Uni inner person, special unity of self, NOT "myself" but "my self"

Una — Uniale parent, title of respect

Una Columb — Ancient Columbia River flowing west to Pacific Ocean

Uni — Abbreviation of uniale, plural = uni's

FACETS of PERCEPTION

Uniale — 3rd sex/gender, embodiment of all M & F genome, able to reproduce all genders

unit dissolution   Family unit dissolved

Virtues of Everdon

PIETAS *(Responsibility)*
OFFICIUM *(Social Obligation)*
CONSTANTIA *(Perseverance)*
GRAVITAS *(Seriousness and Authority)*
AEQUUM *(Balance)*
TRIA IN AETERNNUM *(Forever Three)*
JUCUNDA VITAE *(Joyful Life)*

ACKNOWLEDGMENTS

Appreciation for the photography of J.L. Snyder, the writing analysis by David Mecklenburg, and support of Blue Forge Press and Senior Editor Brianne DiMarco. Discussion and reviews by Jodie Emmons, R.J. Bauer, Patricia Shehan and Beta Readers were constant encouragement.

ABOUT THE AUTHOR

From reading children's books to grade school students, to creating the Senior to Senior Intergenerational Communications project, J.W. Capek has always appreciated the art of storytelling! Growing up in Arizona, teaching high school and raising a family in California, J.W. moved to the Northwest to be an author. Her Deerwhere Codex trilogy creates a world with quantum computers, epigenetics, and three unique genders. J.W.'s short stories span the human experience from tragedy to ridiculous. Check out www.jwcapek.com for current information.

www.ingramcontent.com/pod-product-compliance
Lightning Source LLC
Chambersburg PA
CBHW070340010826
48976CB00017B/558